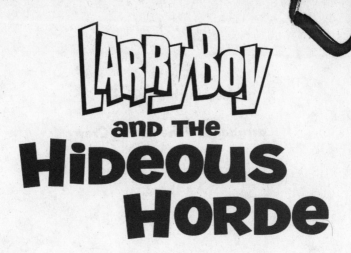

LarryBoy

and the

Hideous Horde

D0949286

Also in this series

Larryboy and the Crusty Crew

Larryboy to the Rescue

3 books in 1

VeggieTales

LarryBoy

and the
Hideous Horde

Sean Gaffney & Bob Katula

ZONDERkidz

VeggieTales

Larryboy

AND THE EMPEROR OF ENVY

WRITTEN BY
SEAN GAFFNEY

ILLUSTRATED BY
MICHAEL MOORE

BASED ON THE HIT VIDEO SERIES: LARRYBOY
CREATED BY PHIL VISCHER
SERIES ADAPTED BY TOM BANCROFT

ZONDERkidz

ZONDERVAN.com/
AUTHORTRACKER
follow your favorite authors

TABLE OF CONTENTS

A CONTENT HEART
IS A HEALTHY HEART.

A HEART AT PEACE
GIVES LIFE TO THE BODY,
BUT ENVY ROTS THE BONES.

-PROVERBS 14:30

CHAPTER 1

SOMETHING ROTTEN IN THE SCHOOL OF BUMBLYBURG

It was a typical day at Bumblyburg's Veggie Valley Elementary School. Well, okay, maybe it wasn't such a typical day. In fact, something just plain weird was going on. The teacher, Mr. Asparagus, was acting a bit oddly.

"Don't you think Mr. Asparagus is acting a bit oddly?" asked Lenny Carrot about his teacher.

"He sure is," said Laura Carrot. "And he looks kind of funny. Like cardboard."

"His lips don't move when he talks," Percy Pea piped in. "That's weird."

"You know," said Renee Blueberry, "he looks a bit like a scallion from the side."

"What do you think, Junior?" asked Laura.

Junior Asparagus didn't know what to think! After all, the teacher was his father. But his dad was acting oddly. And he sure did look funny. Almost as if he was wearing a cardboard mask drawn with crayon.

"Time for a math lesson," squeaked the teacher.

"See!" whispered Percy. "His lips didn't move!"

"That doesn't sound like my dad," said Junior.

The teacher put a black bag on top of his desk. "Now, children," the teacher said, "I want you all to put your milk money into this bag. Then we will play a game."

"What game?" asked Junior.

"Hide-and-Seek," replied the teacher. "You will close your eyes and count to a million while I run and hide. Won't that be fun?"

Junior thought hard. His dad sounded funny, looked as if he was wearing a cardboard mask, talked without moving his lips, and now asked the kids to hand over their milk money for a game of Hide-and-Seek.

"Hey!" shouted Junior. "You aren't my dad! You're the Milk Money Bandit!"

"But I look like your dad, don't you think?" asked the teacher.

"I think you're wearing a mask," said Junior.

"Am not," said the teacher.

"Are too!"

"Am not!"

That moment, a rather large suction cup flew through the open window and plopped onto Mr. Asparagus' face. With a loud *THWOOP*, the plunger was pulled back through the window, ripping off the mask. It was the Milk Money Bandit after all!

"Erk!" shrieked the Bandit.

"I knew it!" exclaimed Junior. "But where did that

plunger come from?"

All the students turned and looked out the window. It was Larryboy! One of his suction-cup ears sported the Milk Money Bandit's mask, and he was trying to shake it loose.

"I am that hero!" Larryboy proclaimed.

Then Larryboy leaped through the open window, tripped on the windowsill, and fell into the classroom, landing on his face.

"I meant to do that," the hero said, popping upright. "Now, Bandit, where is the *real* Mr. Asparagus? Talk now, unless you want the other ear!"

Larryboy leaned threateningly toward the bandit.

"No, not the ears! I'll talk!" howled the villain. "I just wish I had more milk money!"

Larryboy scowled at the bandit.

"Mr. Asparagus is in the closet!" the bandit said, quickly.

Junior ran to the closet and opened the door.

"Dad!"

"Son!"

Junior's dad hopped out of the closet.

"It sure was dark in there," Mr. Asparagus said. "Thank you, Junior."

Mr. Asparagus came out of the closet and looked at the Milk Money Bandit quite sternly. "*You* should learn to be content with the money you have!" he scolded. "Thank *you*, Larryboy, for saving the day!"

Larryboy smiled. "My pleasure," he said. "And now to take care of the bandit!"

CHAPTER 2

I AM THAT HERO!

A short while later, Chief Croswell arrived at the classroom.

"I understand the Milk Money Bandit is ready to be taken to jail," he said.

"As soon as he is done at the blackboard," Larryboy responded.

The bandit was at the board, writing "I will not steal milk money" one thousand times.

"A fitting punishment for his crime," the Chief said.

"And now, my work here is done!" said Larryboy. He jumped out the window, tripping on the sill again, and fell onto the lawn.

"I meant to do that," the hero said as he popped back up.

Then Larryboy hopped into the Larry-Mobile and sped off toward his secret hideout.

Soon, the videophone in the Larry-Mobile began chirping.

"Hello, Archie," said Larryboy. Archibald—Larryboy's assistant, manservant, and technical wizard—appeared on the video screen.

"Well done, Larryboy!" Archibald said. "I monitored the whole thing from the Larry-Cave. You did splendidly."

"Thank you," said Larryboy.

"However, you may wish to be more careful jumping through windows."

"I think my mask throws off my depth perception."

"Well, never mind that now. I called to remind you of

tonight's superhero class."

"Tonight? But tonight is a classic double-feature night at the movies!"

"Well," said Archibald, "what do you think is more important, attending movies or school?"

"But the movies are *Attack of the Rotten Tomato* plus *Salad Wars: Frankencelery Strikes Back*!" exclaimed Larryboy.

Archibald glared at Larryboy through the screen.

"I'm on my way to school! Over and out!" Our hero spun his roadster around and zoomed down the street.

CHAPTER 3

A TYPICAL NIGHT
IN SUPERHERO SCHOOL

Larryboy raced down the hallway of the Bumblyburg Community College, stopping in front of a door with a big sign that read, "Superhero 101: The Basics of Being Super."

"Here it is," Larryboy mumbled to himself. "I hope I'm not late."

Our hero stuck his head inside the doorway. The classroom was filled with superheroes, all sitting and facing the front. Bok Choy, the professor, stood in the front of the class. Larryboy slipped in, hoping not to be noticed. Unfortunately, he also tripped over the Norse superhero's backpack and toppled over a chair.

"Let me interrupt class with a riddle," said Bok Choy. "What do these three things have in common: an overdue library book, a school bus that is behind schedule, and Larryboy? Would the cucumber in the back like to guess?"

"Uhm," sputtered Larryboy.

"They are all *late!*" pronounced his teacher.

"That's a good riddle!" Larryboy said. "What's black, white, and read all over?"

Bok Choy took a deep breath and stared at Larryboy.

"Sorry, I was trying to slip in unnoticed."

"Slip in unnoticed?" Bok Choy asked. "A large cucumber dressed in yellow, sporting a big purple cape, and bumping into chairs in the back row? It's a wonder you were noticed at all. Take your seat, and try not to be late again."

Larryboy slipped into a chair. Bok Choy resumed his lecture.

"As I was saying, envy is a dangerous thing—especially to a superhero! Let's look at this chart showing the effects

of envy on the super body."

Larryboy looked at the superhero sitting next to him. He was a decorated apple, dressed in red, white, and blue. The headdress covering his head had two small wings attached. He also had a marvelous round shield that was painted blue with a big white *A* in the middle.

"Psst," whispered Larryboy. "Howdy. I'm Larryboy, from Bumblyburg. Who are you?"

"American Pie, defender of truth, justice, and vitamin A," American Pie whispered back. "I'm from Tiggety Town. What's the answer to *your* riddle?"

"Oh, that's easy! A Larryboy chapter book!"

"Huh?" American Pie asked curiously.

"Never mind," Larryboy said. "Hey! I sure like the wings on your head. Can you fly?"

"Nope," said the captain. "But they do make me look cool."

"Nifty," said Larryboy.

"Moving right along," Bok Choy urged with authority as he cleared his throat to demand more attention. "I want you all to take out your *Superhero Handbooks* and turn to section 20, paragraph 14, line 30."

"Psst!" Larryboy whispered to American Pie. "Can I look on with you? I left my *Superhero Handbook* in my glove compartment."

"Sure," said his neighbor.

"The book says, 'A heart at peace gives life to the body, but envy rots the bones,'" read Bok Choy. "Envy, also known as jealousy, eats away at you from the inside. It is an evil to avoid!"

Larryboy couldn't concentrate. He kept staring at American Pie's shield.

"That's a really nifty shield," he whispered.

"Thanks," American Pie whispered back.

"Can I hold it for a minute?" asked our hero.

"Okay," said the Pie. "Just be very careful."

Larryboy took the shield. It was heavier than it looked.

"Neat-o," said Larryboy.

"There is only one cure for envy," Bok Choy continued with his lecture. "You must learn to be happy with the things you already have. Instead of wishing you had your neighbor's car, be grateful for your own car. Instead of desiring your neighbor's cat, think of how happy you are with your own dog."

"What if I don't have a dog?" asked the Scarlet Tomato.

"I was just using that as an example," explained Bok Choy.

"My neighbor has a dog," said the tomato. "But I don't." Bok Choy sighed.

"What do *you* have?" asked the teacher.

"A goldfish."

"Can you be content with that?"

"Sure. It's a pretty good goldfish."

"All right then," the teacher continued. "Remember, a content heart is a healthy heart. Repeat that, heroes."

"A content heart is a healthy heart," the class members

repeated—except for Larryboy. He was busy playing with the shield.

Larryboy lifted the disk up and down, playing with the weight in his hands.

"Psst," he whispered. "I bet you can throw this shield about a mile!"

"Perhaps," agreed American Pie. "But not in *here*!"

"It would make a great Frisbee," Larryboy said as he pretended to throw the shield like a Frisbee.

"Be careful!" hissed American Pie.

"Don't worry," said Larryboy. "I'm always careful... oops."

Larryboy wasn't holding on tightly enough. The shield flew around the room, careening off one wall only to ricochet off another.

"What's going on?" demanded Bok Choy.

"Look out!" shouted Electro-Melon.

"My shield!" yelled American Pie.

"Ahhh!" screamed Bok Choy as the shield bounced
to the front of the room, heading straight for him.

He raised the *Superhero Handbook* to block the
flying disk. The shield skimmed over the edge of the book
and shot through Bok Choy's head, giving him a flattop.
The whole class stared at their instructor
for a moment. Finally, Bok Choy broke the silence.

"Class, it looks like Larryboy is more interested in
a different lesson," he said. "It seems he would rather
practice being a barber!"

"Oops," said Larryboy.

CHAPTER 4

ENTER ... THE EMPEROR

Meanwhile, in a secret hideaway on the edge of Bumblyburg, an evil plan was being designed. Not just any evil plan, mind you, but that of Larryboy's nemesis, the Emperor Napoleon of Crime and Other Bad Stuff! The evil cherry tomato was sitting in his throne room when he called in his soldiers.

"Troops! Come in here!" called the villain.

The Emperor's army stumbled into the room. The term *army*, as it turns out, was a bit misleading. In fact, this particular army was really two muscular sweet potatoes named Frank and Jesse.

"And we really aren't that sweet," said Jesse.

"Who are you talking to?" asked Frank.

"Nobody," Jesse responded.

"Listen up, soldiers!"

barked the Emperor. "It's time for me to share with you my plan to conquer all of Bumblyburg!"

"How sweet! I always wished we could do something like that," Jesse exclaimed.

"I've managed to get my hands on a very special formula," the Emperor said. "I call it the Envy Formula!"

With a flourish, the Emperor waved a flask of blue liquid in front of the sweet potatoes.

"Gee, I wish I had an envy formula," Jesse commented.

"I wish *you'd* be quiet!" said Frank.

"Anyone who drinks this formula will be filled with envy. And we all know that envy makes people weak. But with *this* formula, they become super weak," the Emperor continued. "And I plan to see to it that everyone in Bumblyburg gets a taste!"

"That's nice," said Jesse. "Sharing like that is a real nice thing."

"Let me get this straight," said Frank. "Drinking the formula makes a person jealous; and when they get jealous, they get super weak?"

"That's right," answered the villain. "And the more envious they are, the weaker they become! They will feel tired and sluggish. They will hardly be able to move. They will only want to lie down and rest!"

"You know, I'm kind of tired myself," said Jesse.

"Didn't you take a nap this afternoon?" asked Frank.

"Yes, but only a little one."

"Can we get back to the point, please," demanded the

Emperor. "Now then, are there any other questions?"

"Yes," Jesse said. "Are you *really* a tomato?"

The Emperor let out a growl. "Yes, I am a tomato!"

"But aren't you too small to be a tomato?" Jesse asked.

"I've explained this a million times!" the Emperor ranted. "I am a cherry tomato. We are *supposed* to be small."

"So doesn't that make you more of a fruit than a tomato?" asked Jesse.

"Actually," Frank interrupted, "from a strictly scientific standpoint, tomatoes are fruits and not vegetables."

"Really?" asked Jesse. "I don't think I knew that."

"Quiet!" shouted the Emperor. "Are there any more questions about the formula?"

"I have one," said Frank. "How does the formula help us take over Bumblyburg?"

"Simple," the Emperor replied. "Once everyone has taken the formula, they will become envious. When they become envious, they will become weak. And then they will have no strength left to fight us when we take over Bumblyburg! Bwaa-haa-haa-ha!" The Emperor threw back his head and laughed. Frank and Jesse laughed too, although Jesse later admitted he didn't really get the joke.

CHAPTER 5

NEXT DAY AT THE BUMBLE

The next day at the *Daily Bumble*, Bob the editor was fuming mad.

"I'm fuming mad," said Bob.

He was talking to Vicki, the staff photographer. Junior, the cub reporter from Veggie Valley Elementary School, listened in.

"What's got your goat this time, Chief?" asked Vicki. She liked to tease Bob by calling him "Chief." She knew that got his goat. Bob ignored it.

"Mister Slushee, Bumblyburg's very own ice cream shop, is having a Slushee-Slurping contest today," Bob grumbled. "They are giving out free Slushees to the whole town. It will be a major event!"

"Sounds good to me," said Vicki. "So what's your beef?"

"What's my beef? I don't have an available reporter to cover the story, so I have to go myself. I wish I had a reporter available."

"That's not so bad," said Vicki. "I'm going to be there to take photographs."

"But I don't *like* Slushees!" said Bob.

"What's not to like about Slushees?" asked Vicki.

"I get brain-freeze headaches," said Bob.

"Excuse me," Junior cleared his throat. "But I could report on the contest."

"Who's that?" demanded Bob.

"Me, Junior Asparagus, sir!"

"Oh, you," said Bob. "Listen kid, it's great that you're the cub reporter covering stories from Veggie Valley Elementary School, but you're just a kid. You can't cover important stories like the Mister Slushee's Slushee-Slurping Contest. Understand?"

Junior nodded.

"What are you doing here, anyway?" asked the editor.

"I'm turning in my front-page story on Larryboy's capture of the Milk Money Bandit," Junior replied.

Everyone suddenly heard a loud beep, much like that of a microwave oven. Bob looked to the corner of the office where Larry, the janitor, was mopping.

"I didn't notice you there," said Bob.

"Excuse me, but I think your mop is beeping," said Junior.

"Time to mop the closet," Larry said, dashing out of the room.

"Did that cucumber have a timer in his mop?" asked Bob.

"Now *that's* keeping to a tight cleaning schedule!" marveled Vicki.

CHAPTER 6

ARCHIE CALLING

Larry quickly ducked into the hall closet. After checking to make sure he was alone, he stuck his head into the mop. The seemingly plain mop had a video screen built into the strands. Archibald appeared on the screen.

"Hello, Archie," said Larry.

"Greetings, Master Larry," said Archibald. "How is your job at the newspaper?"

"I'm glad you brought that up," said Larry. "I still don't understand why I have to be a janitor. I am a world-famous superhero!"

That was true. For Larry, the janitor, was also Larryboy, the superhero!

"Let me explain it again," said his trusted friend. "By working at the newspaper, you can learn about criminal activity the moment it is reported."

"Couldn't I just watch BNN, the Bumblyburg News Network?"

"And sit around the house all day?" asked Archibald. "No,

being at the *Bumble* is much better."

"Sounds like you are trying to get me out of the house,"
Larry laughed.

"Maybe we should change the subject," Archibald quickly interrupted. "I have important information for you!"

"Me too!" said Larry excitedly. "I learned something really important while cleaning the editor's office."

"I told you the janitor job would pay off," said Archibald.
"What did you learn?"

"They're giving out free Slushees at Mister
Slushee today!"

"Oh, I see," said his partner.

"So what's *your* important information?" asked Larry.

"I wanted to warn you that your archenemy, Emperor
Napoleon of Crime and Other Bad Stuff, has been spotted
near Bumblyburg."

"The Emperor near Bumblyburg? That *is* important news. How did you hear about it?"

"Well, er…" said Archibald. "Actually, I saw it on BNN."

"Hmmm," said Larry. "Well, I had better make plans to deal with the Emperor. And you know what helps a cucumber make good plans?"

"What?" asked Archibald.

"Free Slushees! Toodles!"

Larry clicked off the videophone and pulled the mop off of his head. Whistling, he stepped out of the closet and bounded down the hall. Junior and Vicki were passing by the closet.

"It sounded like the janitor was mumbling to himself in the closet," said Junior.

"He is a strange one," said Vicki. "But he sure is good with a plunger!"

CHAPTER 7

THE PLOT
(AND THE SLUSHEE) THICKENS

It was pandemonium outside Mister Slushee. It seemed as if the entire town was trying to get in for their free Slushees! Chief Croswell blocked the door.

"Hold on, everyone," he said. "You know that Mister Slushee doesn't open for business for another ten minutes. Until that time, we can't let anybody in."

"Ohhhhh!" groaned the crowd.

The Emperor and his henchmen were hiding in the alley next to the Slushee shop.

"Did you hear that?" asked Frank. "With Chief Croswell blocking the door, we can't get into the shop so we can pour the Envy Formula into the Slushee machine, thus ensuring that everyone in Bumblyburg drinks the formula!"

"Good job at bringing the reader up to speed," said Jesse.

"What reader?" asked Frank.

"Never mind that," said the Emperor. "I can get past Chief Croswell. You two stand next to the back door."

"But the door is locked," said Frank.

"I know that," said the Emperor. "I will unlock it from the inside."

"But how will you get past Chief Croswell?" asked Jesse.

"I will use my superpower!" declared the cherry tomato.

"Cool," said Jesse.

"Neat," said Frank.

"What superpower?" asked Jesse.

The Emperor shook his head.

"Weren't you paying attention in supervillain school?" he asked. "All supervillains are either mad geniuses or have superpowers."

"What kind of powers?" asked Frank.

"You know," said the Emperor. "Like super strength, or super speed, or the ability to fly."

"Wow! What's your superpower?"

"When I hold my breath," explained the villain, "I become very, very small."

"You're already are very, very small," said Jesse.

"I become even smaller!" yelled the Emperor. "Watch!"

The Emperor held his breath. Then he began shrinking! Soon he was almost too small to see.

"That *is* small," said Jesse.

"You said it," agreed Frank.

The Emperor let out his breath and grew back to normal size.

"When I'm tiny, I can slip right past Chief Croswell

without being seen."

"You can usually slip by most people without being seen," Jesse observed.

The Emperor growled and said, "Go stand by the back door and wait for me!"

Then he held his breath and shrunk down to a miniscule size. He hopped around the corner and headed for the shop's front door. Chief Croswell was a giant from his point of view!

The Emperor easily slid through underneath the door and into the shop. Once inside, he let out his breath. Back to full size, he gleefully ran and opened the back door.

"Get in here," he said to his henchmen.

Frank and Jesse lumbered into the shop. The Emperor made his way to the Slushee machine. He took out the vial of blue liquid.

"Now, if one of you would be so kind as to pour this vial into the Slushee machine," he said, "then when everyone eats their free Slushees, they will be infected with the Envy Formula!"

"Why don't *you* dump it in?" asked Jesse.

"I'm not tall enough to reach the opening," said the Emperor. "That's why I need your help."

"Why don't you grow back to full size?" asked Jesse.

"I *am* full size," barked the Emperor.

"Why don't I stop talking now," said Jesse.

"That would be a good idea!"

Frank took the vial from the Emperor and poured it into the Slushee machine.

"Good work!" said the Emperor. "Now, let's sneak out the back so no one will suspect a thing. Then all we need to do is wait until everyone has slurped a Slushee. At that moment, we can march on Bumblyburg!"

"Can we stop by my house first?" asked Jesse. "If we're going to be marching, I want to be wearing comfortable shoes."

"Just go!" yelled the Emperor.

Emperor Napoleon of Crime and Other Bad Stuff led his henchmen out the back door, laughing maniacally.

CHAPTER 8

THE SLUSHEE CONTEST

When Chief Croswell opened the doors, the citizens of Bumblyburg stampeded into the shop. Wally helped Herbert work the Slushee machine, pouring out Slushee after Slushee. The shop was packed with vegetables.

"You were right," Vicki said to Bob. "This is a big story."

"I can't believe all these people," Bob said.

"Why not, Chief?" asked Vicki.

"You'd have to be very silly to get this excited about a Slushee contest."

"Look, there's Larry, our janitor," Vicki said.

"My point is proven!"

Larry was sitting with Junior at the far end of the counter.

"This is exciting," said Junior.

"Free Slushees!" said Larry.

"It looks like the whole town is here," said Junior.

"Free Slushees!" said Larry.

"I bet I could write a great story about this," said Junior. "Even if *some* people think I'm not grown up enough to be a real reporter."

"Free Slushees!" responded Larry.

"My dad says God made me special, just the way I am—and that I'll be grown up when I'm good and ready," Junior said. "But I want to be a grown-up right now!"

"Free Slushees!" said Larry.

Chief Croswell hopped onto the counter and tried to get everyone's attention.

"Attention!" he shouted.

Wally let out a loud whistle, and everyone quieted down.

"Thank you, Wally," said the chief. "Welcome to Mister Slushee's Slushee-Slurping Contest. I have been asked to officiate today's event."

"What's 'o-fish-he-ate'?" asked Larry.

"'O-fish-she-ate.' It means 'judge,'" said Junior.

"Poor fish," said Larry.

"Everyone who wants to compete must sit at the counter," explained the chief.

Herbert and Wally had finished filling up the counter with cup after cup of Slushee. They moved away from the Slushee machine and squeezed into two chairs. Larry and Junior already had seats, as did Officers Boysen and Blue, Laura, Lenny, and several others.

"You should compete!" encouraged Vicki.

"Don't be silly," said Bob.

"It's a great idea," Vicki said, with a wink. "Get a first-hand angle for the story."

"But I always get a brain freeze," Bob complained.

"Come on," Vicki teased. "A little Slushee isn't going to hurt you. Besides, if you eat it slowly enough, you won't get a headache."

"Eat slowly in a slurping contest?"

"Get up there, big guy." Vicki nudged Bob up to the counter.

"Okay, contestants," announced Chief Croswell. "When I say, 'Go,' grab a Slushee cup and start slurping! When you finish a cup, take another. When this alarm clock beeps, the contest will be over! Any questions?"

"Where are the straws?" asked Bob.

Laughter rang through the shop.

"There are no straws in a Mister Slushee Slushee-Slurping Contest," explained the chief. "Just stick your face into the Slushee and slurp."

"But isn't that a little messy?" asked Bob.

"Ready?" asked the chief.

"Couldn't I at least get a spoon?" moaned Bob.

"Set," the chief called.

"This is so embarrassing," said Bob.

"Slurp!" shouted Chief Croswell.

The contestants stuck their faces into their Slushee cups. Bob sighed, pursed his lips, puckered up, and put his face to a cup.

"While they race, the rest of us also get to enjoy Slushees too" said Chief Croswell. "Free Slushees for everyone!"

The chief hopped to the back of the counter and started filling Slushee cups. He passed the cups around until everyone in the shop was busy slurping.

CHAPTER 9

TEN MINUTES LATER,
OR "I DON'T BELIEVE I SLURPED THE
WHOLE THING!"

BEEP!

The alarm clock on the
counter went off. Larry's head shot up.
"Hello, Archie?" he said.

"Time!" Chief Croswell called out.

The contestants lifted their heads from their
Slushees. They all had multicolored stains on their
faces. Chief Croswell moved down the counter,
counting empty Slushee cups.

"Five Slushees for Larry! Three for Junior! Six for
the Berry brothers, Officers Boysen and Blue!"

The Berry brothers smiled a raspberry-strawberry
and banana-grape smile.

"Only one for Bob," announced Chief Croswell.

"And I still got a headache," he grumbled.

"Sixteen for Herbert!"

"Sixteen?" asked Larry. "That's a lot of Slushee!"

"Wait," said Chief Croswell. Wally might have
more empty cups."

The chief counted and then recounted, holding

each cup up to make sure it was empty.

"Seventeen cups! Wally wins!"

"Hooray!" shouted the crowd.

"Urp!" belched Wally.

The chief pulled a large trophy from behind the counter.

"Wally, in honor of your amazing appetite, I award you this Mister Slushee Slushee-Slurping Trophy!"

He handed the trophy to Wally.

"I wish I had a big trophy like Wally," said Herbert.

"Me too," said Officers Boysen and Blue.

"I would be much happier with a trophy like his," said

Officer Blue.

"Not as happy as *I* would be!" insisted Officer Boysen.

"You know what would make *me* happier?" asked Bob. "If I had a lot of reporters on my staff, like all the big-town papers have."

"Where did that come from?" asked Vicki.

"I don't know," said Bob. "It just came out."

"Well, come to think of it," Vicki continued, "I would be happier if I had a brand-new digital camera, like the big-shot photographers have."

Suddenly everybody started talking at once.

"I wish I had a pony, like Margo has," said Laura.

"I want Harry's new Larryboy action figure," said Lenny.

"I wish I was grown up like, well, like grown-ups," whined Junior.

The whole shop was full of "I wish" and "I want" and "I'd rather." Envy was filling the shop! Suddenly, the door burst open and a loud laugh was heard. The crowd shushed and turned to the door. There, in the doorway, they saw ...

Nothing.

CHAPTER 10

THE EMPEROR'S ENTRANCE

"Down here! I'm down here!"

Everyone shifted their gaze down and saw the Emperor standing on the threshold!

"I have come to take over Bumblyburg," announced the Emperor.

The crowd looked at the small menace and began laughing.

"Oh, yeah?" said Chief Croswell. "You and what army?"

"Me and this army," said the villain as he stepped aside to make room for his henchmen.

Frank and Jesse lumbered in through the door.

"*Those* two? *They're* your army?" chuckled Bob.

Everyone laughed again.

"Officers Boysen and Blue," said Chief Croswell, "take these scoundrels into custody."

"I wish I had an army

like you have," said Officer Blue.

"Even a couple of deputies would be nice," agreed Officer Boysen.

"Boysen! Blue!" snapped the chief.

"Right! You are all under arrest!" Officer Blue pronounced. But as he stepped forward, he stumbled and fell to the floor, with Office Boysen stumbling right behind him.

"What's wrong with the Berry brothers?" asked Junior.

"I don't know," said a stunned Officer Boysen.

"I don't feel very good," Blue mumbled from the floor.

"I don't feel very good either," said Herbert.

"Do you think it's from slurping too many Slushees?" asked Wally.

"You can *never* have too many Slushees," Herbert replied.

"Hah!" gloated the Emperor. "You are all too weak to stand up to me! You laugh at my height! You laugh at my army! Well, who's laughing now?"

"You are, boss," said Jesse.

"I know I am. That's my point."

"Oh."

"To make sure no one interferes, my troops will tuck you all safely away in jail. Then Bumblyburg will be mine! While you sit in jail wishing for things you can't have, I am going to make all *my* wishes come true!"

"Wait!" said Chief Croswell weakly. "Aren't you forgetting about Larryboy? When he hears about this, you will be sorry!"

At the far end of the counter, Larry began thinking.

I wish I *was Larryboy,* he mused to himself. "Wait a minute. I am that hero!"

Larry hopped off his chair and snuck out through the back door.

CHAPTER 11

GOOD BATTLES EVIL

"Stop, vile villain!"

Larryboy shouted.

He had reemerged from the back alley.

He was now dressed in his full Larryboy costume. The Emperor and his henchmen froze.

"What do we do now?" asked Jesse.

"He doesn't look weak," said Frank. "What if he didn't have any Slushees?"

The Emperor looked worried for a moment. Then he smiled.

"Look at his face, boys," he said.

Larryboy had a red-purple-green Slushee stain around his mouth!

"Okay, superhero," the Emperor said. "You got me. Before you take me in, may I ask you a question?"

"Sure," said Larryboy.

"Isn't there anything that someone else has that you wish you had?" asked the villain. "Like a toy, or a car, or a special skill?"

"A kitty-cat, maybe?" suggested Frank.

"Or an octopus?" added Jesse.

"Octopus?" asked Frank.

"I like octopuses," said Jesse.

"Don't you mean octopi?" asked Frank.

"No thanks," said Jesse. "I don't like pie. But I do wish I had a piece of cake."

"Gentlemen, please!" shouted the Emperor. "Well, Larryboy? Can't you think of anything?"

Larryboy thought for a moment.

"Now that you mention it," he said, "I would like to have a shield like American Pie has. That was nifty. Round and sturdy. And boy, that thing could fly!"

"Ahem." Vicki cleared her throat. "Larryboy, aren't you

in the middle of doing something important?"

"That's right," said Larryboy. "Okay, villains, let's go!"

"I've changed my mind," smirked the Emperor. "You will have to take us by force."

"Alright, if that's the way you want it."

Larryboy stepped forward, cocked his head, and let fly a mighty super-suction ear!

Only the ear didn't fly. It fizzled, actually, and fell to the floor at Larryboy's feet.

"I feel funny," the hero said. "And I'm too weak to shoot my ears right!"

The Emperor laughed. And laughed. And laughed.

CHAPTER 12

NINETY-NINE BOTTLES OF SLUSHEE ON THE WALL

"In you go," said Jesse.

The Emperor's henchmen were escorting Herbert and Wally into a cell at the Bumblyburg prison.

"That's the last of them," said Frank. "The whole town, all in jail."

"Can't we at least have something to drink? I want something to drink!" whined Officers Boysen and Blue.

"There's ninety-nine bottles of Slushee on the wall," Frank pointed out.

"Yeah. Just take one down, pass it around," added Jesse.

"Ninety-eight bottles of Slushee on the wall," finished Frank.

"Hey, that would make a great song!" Jesse realized.

"Hey, sweet potato!"

Wally was yelling at them through the bars. He and Herbert were both sitting on the cots in the cell.

"Tell Herbert to give me his cot," Wally yelled. "It's softer than mine!"

"I'm too tired to switch cots," said Herbert. "Besides, I want his cot. It's firmer than mine!"

"Boy, I hope that Envy Formula wears off soon," said Frank. "These gourds are driving me crazy!"

The two henchmen walked out of the prison. A few cells down, Bob, Junior and Larryboy were sharing a cell.

"I feel super weak," Junior said.

"Me too," said Bob. "And my head hurts."

"Well," said Larryboy, "I feel weak, my head hurts, and

there is a ringing in my ears."

"That's because your ears *are* ringing," said Bob.

"They are?" Larryboy sat up on his cot. "Hello? Archie, is that you?"

"Hello, Larryboy!"

Larryboy could hear Archibald's voice through the radio set in his headdress. Bob and Junior, who couldn't

hear Archibald, looked on confused.

"Archie, am I glad to hear your voice," said Larryboy. "I'm in jail!"

"Oh, no," said Archibald. "I told you to slow down when driving through town!"

"It's not that," said Larryboy. "It's Emperor Napoleon of Crime and Other Bad Stuff!"

"Why are you telling *us* that?" asked Bob.

"I'm not talking to you," said Larryboy.

"You're not talking to me?" asked Archie.

"Yes, I'm talking to you," said Larryboy. "I'm not talking to Bob."

"Are you talking to *me*?" asked Junior.

"No, I'm talking to Archie," said the superhero.

Bob and Junior looked around the cell.

"He must be invisible," said Bob.

"I wish I had an invisible friend," said Junior.

"Archie isn't invisible," explained Larryboy. "You just can't see him."

"I wish I had a friend who wasn't invisible but you just couldn't see him," said Junior.

"Never mind explaining," Archibald pushed on. "Just tell me what happened."

So Larryboy told Archibald about the Mister Slushee Slushee-Slurping Contest, the Emperor's entrance, Officers Boysen and Blue becoming ill, and his own brief battle with the villain.

"And that's how we ended up here," said Larryboy.

"It's unbelievable, but I'm too weak to try to escape! I wish I was back home, like you."

"Keep your courage up, my friend," said Archibald. "I will go down to Mister Slushee and investigate. Maybe I can find out what is making so many people lose their strength!"

"Good idea, Archie," said Larryboy. "And while you're doing that, I'm going to lie down on my cot and dream that I had a mattress that wasn't lumpy. Over and out."

Larryboy sunk down on his cot and commenced dreaming.

CHAPTER 13

THE EMPEROR'S NEW BUMBLYBURG

"Lower!" shouted the Emperor.

The evil cherry tomato was standing in the large doorway to the Mister Slushee shop.

"I said lower!" he yelled again.

A loud **CRUNCH** rang out. Suddenly, the doorway to Mister Slushee was the ideal size for the short villain!

"That's perfect," said the Emperor. "Now on to the next building!"

Frank and Jesse stood next to the crank of a really huge, super gigantic, massively gargantuan vise grip. The vise was clamped down on the Mister Slushee shop. They had scrunched down the entire building to fit the Emperor!

"And it was really hard work," Jesse said.

"What was really hard work?" asked Frank.

"Scrunching down the entire building to fit the Emperor," said Jesse.

"What are you telling me for?" asked Frank.

"I know it was really hard work. I stood right here and scrunched with you."

"I'm not telling you," Jesse said. "I'm telling the reader."

"Oh ... right!"

"Come along, men," the Emperor called. "We have a lot more scrunching to do!"

Frank and Jesse marched away from the Mister Slushee shop.

"Now that the buildings are being scrunched down to the Emperor's size," said Jesse, "how will *we* be able to stand up in them?"

"Quiet," said Frank. "Or the Emperor might decide to scrunch us down, too!"

As they left, Archibald tiptoed around the corner, wriggled his way through the door, and crawled into the building.

CHAPTER 14

ALFRED REPORTS BACK

BRRRING! BRRRING!

Larryboy sat up on his cot.

"Am I late for work again?" he asked.

"It's your ears," said Bob. "They're ringing again."

"Oh, excuse me," Larryboy said. "That's my radio hidden in my super-suction ears."

"I wish I had a radio," said Bob.

"I wish I had super-suction ears," said Junior.

"I wish I had a radio *and* super-suction ears!" exclaimed Larryboy.

"*You do*," Bob reminded him. "And they're still ringing.

"Right," said Larryboy. "Hello, Alfred?"

"Larryboy, I found something interesting. I took a very interesting sample from the Slushee machine."

"I wish I had a Slushee," said Larryboy.

"Did it taste good?"

"I didn't eat it," said Archibald. "I

took it to the lab and ran some tests. The Slushees were tainted with what appears to be an envy formula."

"An envy formula," repeated Larryboy.

"What's he saying?" asked Bob.

"The Slushees were tainted with an envy formula," said the superhero. "I seem to recall someone talking about envy recently. If only I could remember where."

"Was it someone at Mister Slushee?" asked Archibald.

"How about someone you passed on the street?" asked Junior.

"Was it a used-car salesman?" suggested Bob.

"No, none of those."

"At the Veggie Valley Elementary School," Junior said, "our teacher once taught us about envy."

"That's it!" shouted Larryboy. "School!"

"You go to the Veggie Valley Elementary School, too?" asked Junior.

"No, but in my night class, Professor Bok Choy talked about envy. He said that envy rots the bones."

"There did seem to be a lot of jealousy at Mister Slushee," said Junior. "And after everyone became envious, we all started to feel weak. Envy caused our weakness!"

"I wish I had thought of that," said Bob.

"That's it!" said Archibald. "And God doesn't want us to be envious of others! No wonder you couldn't fight the Emperor!"

"So what do I do? What do I do?" asked Larryboy.

"To counteract the formula, you must stop being envious," said Archibald. "Then your strength will return."

"I can do that! Then I'll take care of the Emperor and his cronies. But how will I get out of this cell?"

"I wish I had the keys to this cell," said Junior.

"Of course, the keys!" Larryboy exclaimed.

"Why not just use your super-suction ears to get them?" asked Bob as they all gazed at the set of keys hanging on the far wall outside of the cell.

"They're all the way across the room! I don't know if I have the strength to shoot my super-suction ears that far," moaned Larry.

"Larryboy," Archibald said over the radio. "Simply stop being envious, and then you should have enough power to reach them."

"Oh! Of course!" Larryboy agreed. "I am the happiest cucumber alive! I'm happy with everything I have! I'm happy just being ..."

"Larryboy, you have a job to do!" Archibald reminded him.

"Right! Over and out!"

Larryboy stood up and wiggled an ear between the bars. Then he took aim, and *POP!* The plunger zoomed across the room, sticking to the keys. With a whir, Larryboy reeled his plunger back in, dragging the keys to the cell.

The superhero turned to face his friends as he tried to yank the keys through the bars. But his ear jammed between the bars, causing him to fall to the floor.

"Oops! I think they're stuck!" he admitted.

Bob and Junior helped Larryboy pull his ear back through the bars to retrieve the keys. Quickly, he unlocked the cell door.

"I'm off to see the Emperor," he proclaimed. "Who's with me?"

"I wish I had your energy," Bob said, "but helping you with those keys zapped every bit I had. I'm still too weak to leave."

"Me too," said Junior.

"You will have to go alone, Master Larry," said Archibald. "Just remember, don't be envious!"

CHAPTER 15

IF AT FIRST YOU DON'T SUCCEED ...

SCRUNCH!

"A little lower!"

The Emperor was standing in the doorway to the Bumblyburg Bank. Frank and Jesse were working the crank of the really huge, super gigantic, massively gargantuan vise that now clamped the bank.

"Halt! Stop that!"

Larryboy was on the scene. He stood defiantly in the middle of the street, facing the bank.

"Oh, look boys," the Emperor chuckled. "Guess who escaped from his cell?"

"Oh, I love riddles," said Jesse. "Did Officers Boysen and Blue escape?"

"No!" grumbled the Emperor.

"Do you really like riddles?" Larryboy asked the sweet potatoes. "'Cuz I have a really good one. What's purple and white and read?..."

"It's Larryboy!" the Emperor interrupted.

"Can't you see?"

"I thought it might be a trick question," said Jesse.

"I wanted to hear the end of the riddle," added Frank.

"Army, attack!" ordered the Emperor.

Frank and Jesse abandoned the crank and headed right for Larryboy.

"Larryboy, can you hear me?" Archibald called through the radio set.

"Loud and clear," said the hero.

"This would be a good time to test the new weapon that I installed in your left super-suction ear."

"The Maypole Ear? But it's not May, it's October."

"That's quite alright, Master Larry. Use it anyway."

"Who's he talking to?" asked Jesse.

"I don't know," replied Frank. "But watch out, he's getting ready to launch a plunger!"

POP! Larryboy's left super-suction ear flew through the air and landed on the ground between the two henchmen.

"Ha! He missed," gloated Frank.

"Maybe," said Larryboy. "Maybe not."

"Uh, Frank," said Jesse. "The plunger is making noise."

Indeed, the plunger was whirring. Suddenly, a tall pole rose up out of the center of it.

"What's that?" asked Frank, staring up at the pole.

A small *POP* resounded from the top of the pole, and two smaller plungers dropped down near the sweet potatoes. *PLOP! PLOP!* The mini-plungers landed squarely on each henchman's head.

"I don't like the sound of this," said Frank.

"Hey, I'm flying!" said Jesse.

The mini-plungers were being reeled to the top of the pole, carrying Jesse and Frank along with them.

"Help!" called Jesse.

"We're stuck up here," yelled Frank.

"Works like a charm," said Larryboy.

"Thank you," said Archibald.

"And now for the big guy," said Larryboy, looking down at his small adversary. "I mean, the little guy."

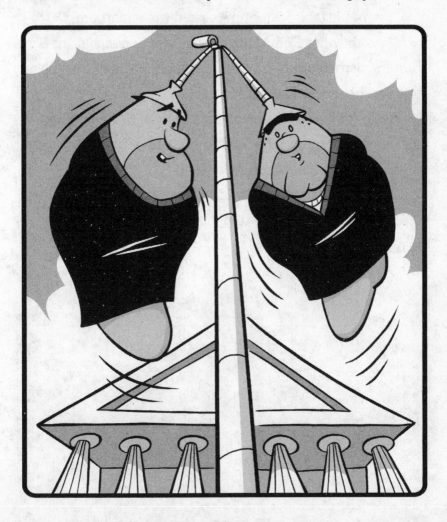

"Wait a minute," said the villain. "May I ask you something?"

"Oh no you don't!" said Larryboy.

"How about the shield that American Pie has? Wouldn't you like that?" taunted the Emperor.

"I'm not listening!" answered the superhero. "La, la, la, la, la, la, la!"

"Other superheroes can fly. Don't you wish you could fly?" the Emperor taunted.

"I'm not listen... fly, huh?" asked the superhero.

"Plus they have other wonderful toys. Remember that Norse superhero with the magic hammer? Wouldn't you like to have a hammer like him?"

"Gee, if I had a hammer," said Larryboy, "I could hammer in the morning. That would be cool. Why can't I have a hammer like that other superhero?"

Larryboy suddenly felt himself getting weaker.

"Oh, no!" he cried. "I don't know how to stay unenvious!"

CHAPTER 16

THE BUMBLYBURG PRISON BLUES

Back at the prison cell, Junior sat on his bunk in a bad mood.

"Hrumpf!" he cried.

"What's on your mind?" asked Bob.

"No matter how hard I try to not envy grown-ups, I don't feel any stronger," Junior replied. "I guess I just can't do it."

"Envy grown-ups?" Bob asked. "Why would you do something silly like that?"

"Grown-ups get to do all kinds of things that I can't. Like be real reporters. And stay up late. And eat nothing but macaroni and cheese for breakfast, lunch, and dinner."

"Still," reasoned Bob, "you get to do a lot of really cool things, too."

"Like what?" Junior was being a little grumpy.

"Well, you get to be cub reporter. Sure, I might not let you cover every story, but how many of the other kids you know get to have their stories published at all?"

"That's true," said Junior.

"And you get to play at recess. I haven't had recess since I was your age."

"Really?" asked Junior. "I do like recess."

"And you get to go to the movies for half-price. I can't go to the movies for half-price."

"My grandpa goes to the movies for half-price," replied Junior. "I bet it won't be long before you can, too."

"I'm *not* as old as your grandpa!" scowled Bob.

"You're not?" asked Junior.

"Let's change the subject," said Bob. "The point is, you can go to movies for half-price now."

"Yeah," said Junior. "I guess being a kid isn't so bad."

"More than that," said Bob. "Being Junior Asparagus isn't so bad."

"Yeah, I like being me!" agreed Junior. "Besides, I learned that little guys can do big things, too! I guess I was forgetting all about that! Hold it, I'm feeling stronger. In fact, I don't feel sick at all!"

"Really? That's probably because you

did more than stop being jealous. You were also content with what you have and who you are," Bob added.

"Yeah! The only way to really stop envy is by being content. A content heart is a healthy heart!" Junior pronounced.

"You said it, kid. And I'll print *that* in my paper any day!" Bob said.

"Oh, my! I'd better go," Junior shouted. "Larryboy doesn't know how to stop envy!"

CHAPTER 17

JUNIOR TO THE RESCUE

"Larryboy?"

"Yes, Archie?" Larryboy responded through his radio set.

"What is that strange sound I'm hearing?"

"What sound, Archie?"

"Well, it's sort of a scrunching and crunching sound."

"Oh, that," said Larryboy. "That would be my head."

"What?"

"Not now, Archie. I'm a little busy."

Larryboy was tied up and standing in the middle of the really huge, super gigantic, massively gargantuan vise. And the clamp was squeezing down on his head! Frank and Jesse had taken the vise off the bank, and they were now using it on Larryboy.

"Now you will know what it feels like to be short," the Emperor gloated.

"Is that what all this is about? *Your* wish to be tall? I don't suppose you would like to be stretched instead?" asked Larryboy.

"No."

"You really should consider it. Of course, you'd look more like a bell pepper. But you're always grouchy, so a pepper sorta suits you. I think you should consider it. Don't ya think?"

"Larryboy!" Junior was racing down the street toward the hero, yelling at the top of his lungs. It isn't enough to not be envious!"

"Hah!" said Jesse. "He learned that three chapters ago!"

"Could you guys hold it down for a second?" asked Larryboy. "I'm trying to hear Junior."

"Oh, sorry," said the sweet potatoes in unison.

"It's just like my dad said!" shouted Junior. "God made each of us special. And God wants us to be happy with who we are and what we have. That's how you defeat envy—by being content!"

"I can do that!" said Larryboy. "If I only knew what 'content' means."

"It means being happy with what you have, rather than wishing for things that others have!"

"Hey," said Jesse. "The kid's got a good point."

"Stop him!" yelled the Emperor. "He'll ruin everything!"

Frank, Jesse, and the Emperor ran toward Junior. The cub reporter spun around and darted the other way. But the potatoes and the Emperor were close behind.

"Help!" yelled Junior.

As they disappeared down the street, Larryboy was left

alone with his thoughts.

Be content, eh? Happy with what I have? Well, it is true that I don't have a cool shield. But I do have other nifty things, like super-suction ears.

And I have Archie, who makes me cool stuff. And I get to live in Bumblyburg with some of the nicest vegetables you could ever hope to call friends. It is good to be Larryboy!

Larryboy stood up tall and proud. He flexed his cucumber muscles; and the ropes around him burst; and the really huge, super gigantic, massively gargantuan vise snapped in half!

"I AM THAT HERO!" Larryboy cried.

CHAPTER 18

TRY, TRY AGAIN

Down the street, Frank, Jesse, and the Emperor surrounded Junior.

"So," taunted the Emperor. "You think a little kid like yourself is going to outwit the Emperor?"

"I'm not so little," said Junior, defiantly. "I'm taller than you."

"He has a point there," agreed Jesse.

"Quiet!" shouted the Emperor. "Grab the kid, and let's get back to squishing Larryboy!"

"Did somebody mention my name?" Larryboy leaped into the middle of the gang, landing next to Junior.

"How did you escape from the vise?" asked Frank.

"Never mind that," said the Emperor. "It won't take much

to make him weak again."

"Oh, yeah?" said Larryboy.

"Yeah," the cherry tomato responded. "Think for a minute, Larryboy. Wouldn't you like to have a nice shield?"

"Sure, who wouldn't?" said the superhero. "But I am pretty happy with the stuff I do have, like these nifty super-suction ears."

"Yeah, but other heroes can fly. Wouldn't you like to be able to fly?"

"That would be fun. But you know what? I already fly with my Larry-Jet. So I'm okay with not being able to fly."

"Drat!" mumbled the Emperor.

"You've defeated envy!" Junior shouted.

"That's right, thanks to you," said Larryboy.

"But you haven't defeated *me* yet!" cried the Emperor. "Army, attack!"

"But, Emperor," Jesse whined, "he isn't weak anymore."

"I've got an idea," said Frank.

"What?" asked Jesse.

"Run!"

Frank and Jesse ran down the street. Larryboy aimed an ear towards them and **POP!** One of his super-suction ears flew down the street. The plunger zoomed past the two potatoes and landed on a billboard advertising Mister Slushee.

"Hah!" shouted Frank. "He missed!"

"You know," said Jesse, "the last time we thought he missed, he didn't really miss."

"What are you trying to say?" asked Frank.

"I guess I'm trying to say, 'Look out!'" hollered Jesse.

Larryboy reeled in his plunger, which uprooted the billboard and pulled it right toward the two henchmen.

WAP! The billboard and the henchmen collided. Frank and Jesse fell to the ground in a daze.

"That ought to keep them quiet for a little bit," said Larryboy. "And now for the ringleader!"

"I still have an ace up my sleeve!" said the Emperor.

"Hah!" crowed Larryboy. "You don't even have sleeves!"

"It's just an expression," said the Emperor. "Watch!"

The Emperor held his breath and nearly shrunk out of sight!

"Oh, no!" cried Junior. "He'll get away!"

"Don't worry," said Larryboy. "Archie thought the Emperor might try to use his super-shrinking power. That's why he packed this!"

Larryboy pulled a handheld Larry-Vacuum from his utility belt. He turned on the vacuum, which sucked dust and debris into its bag. After a minute, Larry turned the vacuum off.

"Now what?" asked Junior.

"Now we wait until the Emperor can't hold his breath anymore."

POOF!

Suddenly a bulge the size and shape of a cherry tomato appeared inside the vacuum bag.

"Looks like we caught the Emperor after all," said Larryboy.

"Thank you for saving the day, Larryboy!" said Junior.

"Thank you, Junior, for showing me how to defeat envy."

BRRRRRING!

"That would be for me," said Larryboy. "Hello, Archie?"

"Larryboy! Are you okay?"

"Thanks to Junior and you, I'm fine."

"And what about the Emperor?"

"Don't worry, Archie. I've got that one in the bag!"

CHAPTER 19

ALL'S WELL THAT ENDS

SKRITCH!

A really huge, super gigantic, massively gargantuan car jack was placed in the doorway of the Bank of Bumblyburg. Several citizens were working the lever, returning the height of the building to its normal size. Chief Croswell, Junior, and Larryboy watched from down the street.

"Soon all of the buildings will be back to their normal sizes," said the chief. "And all of Bumblyburg's citizens have been examined by the doctor. All traces of the Envy Formula are gone!"

"That *is* good news," said Larryboy.

"We sure learned a good lesson, didn't we?" asked Junior.

"That's right," said Larryboy. "Don't mess with Larryboy!"

"Oh, I was thinking of a different lesson," said Junior.

"I know just what you're thinking," said

Larryboy. "Free Slushees aren't all they're cracked up to be."

"Uhm, that isn't it, either" said Junior.

"Don't throw a shield in a classroom?" suggested Larryboy.

"That's good advice," said Junior. "But still, it's not what I was thinking. What is the big thing we learned in this adventure?"

"The prison cots are lumpy?"

"I was thinking more along the lines of being content with what we have," sighed Junior.

"Right! That, too!" agreed the superhero, "Well, I must be off."

Larryboy hopped into his waiting Larry-Mobile. He fired up the engine and drove down the street. Chief Croswell and Junior waved.

As Larryboy came to a stop at the traffic light, a hotrod painted with yellow and red flames pulled up alongside him. The light changed, and the hotrod took off.

"Boy, it sure would be nice to have a car like that," Larryboy said to himself. "But then again, the car I've got isn't too bad!"

Larryboy laughed as he pushed the special button on his dashboard. Suddenly, wings popped out of the side of the Larry-Mobile. The car lifted up into the air, and Larryboy zoomed off into the sky.

VeggieTales

LARRYBOY

AND THE AWFUL EAR WACKS ATTACKS

WRITTEN BY
BOB KATULA

ILLUSTRATED BY
MICHAEL MOORE

BASED ON THE HIT VIDEO SERIES: LARRYBOY
CREATED BY PHIL VISCHER
SERIES ADAPTED BY TOM BANCROFT

ZONDERkidz

TABLE OF CONTENTS

CHAPTER 1

THE GIANT SLIME MONSTER

It was an average day in
Bumblyburg. The leaves were rustling
on the trees, the birds were perched on
the statues in the park, and Bumblyburg's
own superhero, Larryboy, was on patrol.

Larryboy was slowly driving the Larry-Mobile
around the city, looking for signs of crime or other
superhero-needing situations. Normally, Larryboy
liked going on patrol. But today, he was bored.

"I am sooo bored!" he said. "There's nothing happening today … except for the situation with the birds
and the statues. But I'm not going to intervene in that!
If I don't see some sorta trouble soon, I'm gonna go
home and make myself a big peanut-butter sandwi…"

The Larry-Mobile screeched to a halt. Larryboy
saw something coming over the hill, and he couldn't
believe his eyes.

A great big slimy purple blob was creeping over
the hill, wiggling menacingly as it came.

"Oh, peanut brittle!" said Larryboy. "It's a

giant purple slime monster!!"

Right then, Larryboy would have attacked the giant purple slime monster in an effort to save Bumblyburg from its vicious slimy attacks. He would have attacked, except for one thing: Larryboy was scared of giant purple slime monsters.

So instead, Larryboy parked the Larry-Mobile and jumped into the bushes to hide as the giant purple slime monster came over the hill.

"Bumblyburg is doomed!" Larryboy thought to himself. "We need a superhero or something to stop it!"

Then, with horror, Larryboy realized something. "Wait …I…am…that…hero. Drat."

Even though he was afraid, he had to try to stop the giant purple slime monster. Bumblyburg depended on him!

So, as the giant purple slime monster passed the bushes where Larryboy was hiding, he closed his eyes, gritted his teeth, and fired one of his plunger ears.

"Hey!" said the giant purple slime monster. "I've been plungerized!"

This startled Larryboy. He didn't expect the giant purple slime monster to talk. Besides, it didn't sound *anything* like a giant purple slime monster should sound.

"Help! Get this plunger off me! I can't see!" it said.

Then Larryboy realized something: The giant purple slime monster didn't sound like a giant purple slime monster. It sounded like Wally!

Larryboy looked up from behind the bushes, and this is what he saw: Herbert and Wally carrying the largest plate of grape-flavored gelatin he had ever seen.

Larryboy rushed from the bushes and released Wally from his plunger ear. Herbert and Wally explained that they had filled the city swimming pool with grape gelatin, and now they were taking the whole thing home to eat. They didn't even seem to mind that there was a pair of swim fins and a life preserver suspended in the middle of the giant gelatin mold.

"Wow," said Larryboy. "That's a lot of gelatin!"

CHAPTER 2

MUSHROOM AMUCK

This would have probably been the yummiest day of Herbert and Wally's life, except for what happened next.

As Larryboy stood admiring the huge purple blob of gelatin, young Angus Mushroom zoomed up on a scooter, going way too fast!

"Coming through!" shouted Angus.

Larryboy jumped out of the way just in time. But when he jumped aside, he bumped into Wally, causing the giant gelatin to wobble and jiggle dangerously.

"WHOOOOOOAH!" said Herbert and Wally as they tried not to drop the wiggly purple glob.

"Hold on!" said Larryboy. "If I can just activate my gelatin stabilizer device ..."

But it was too late. Herbert and Wally lost control of the gelatin and dropped it right on Larryboy. Larryboy was a

sticky, purple mess. On top of that, he was stuck in a life preserver.

"Are you okay?" asked Herbert.

"Of course I'm okay," said Larryboy. "It takes more than getting mucked up with gelatin to stop a super-hero! But Angus Mushroom might cause more accidents if I don't stop *him*!"

Larryboy got up and hopped over to the Larry-Mobile where he pulled out a rocket-powered skateboard and a helmet. "Traffic violation! This is a job for the Larry-Board!" he said.

With that, Larryboy, covered in purple gelatin and
with a life preserver around his waist, hopped onto
the skateboard and took off after Angus. Problem was,
Larryboy wasn't so good at skateboarding.

"WHOOOOAH DOGGIE!" he said as he whooshed after Angus.

In seconds, the rocket-powered Larry-Board caught up
to Angus, and Larryboy rode beside him. "Stop! Stop!"
said Larryboy.

"Scott?" said Angus with a confused expression. "My
name's Angus, not Scott."

"I know," said Larryboy. "But you have to..."

WHAM!

Larryboy was so busy trying to get Angus to stop that he didn't notice Pa Grape walking along the sidewalk carrying a barrel of Mexican jumping beans. Larryboy crashed into the barrel, sending jumping beans everywhere...including down his spandex superhero suit.

"Hey!" said Pa Grape. "You spilled my jumping beans!"

"Sorry," said Larryboy, "but I gotta go stop Angus before he causes more accidents."

So, Larryboy got back on his Larry-Board and zoomed off after Angus, covered in gelatin, a life preserver around his tummy, and Mexican jumping beans in his suit.

Larryboy caught up to Angus and his scooter again. "Halt!" he said.

"Malt?" said Angus. "I'd love a chocolate malt!"

"No, no," said Larryboy.

WHAM!

Again, Larryboy wasn't looking where he was going. So he didn't see the big hat display out front of the lady's clothing store. He crashed right into it, sending hats everywhere...including a big flowery one that landed on his head.

But Larryboy knew he had to stop Angus before he caused any more accidents. So he kept on going...covered in grape gelatin, a life preserver around his waist, Mexican jumping beans in his suit, and a lady's hat on his head that covered his eyes.

Then he ran smack into a wall.

"Ouch," he said.

Fortunately for Larryboy, Chief Croswell had volun-
teered to fill-in for the school crossing guard that day.
He was just about to help Junior Asparagus cross the
street when he saw Angus coming on his scooter, going
way too fast. Chief Croswell held up his 'stop' sign and
yelled, **"STOP!"**

Angus read the 'stop' sign and finally came to a stop.

"Why does everyone keep calling me Scott?" he asked.

Moments later, Larryboy rocked up on the Larry-Board...and ran into a mailbox.

"Ouch," he said.

By now, the jumping beans in his suit were really starting to tickle. He leapt off his Larry-Board and began jumping around as if his suit was on fire.

Chief Croswell and Junior Asparagus looked at Larryboy who was jumping around wildly, covered in purple gelatin, wearing a life preserver around his waist and a lady's hat on his head. "Are you okay, Larryboy?" Junior asked.

"Yeah," said Larryboy. "Why do you ask?"

CHAPTER 3

TAFFY, BUT NO LAFFY

As Chief Croswell tried to sort things out, a dark figure watched from a nearby alley, doing his best to cloak himself in darkness.

This dark figure was Larryboy's arch enemy, Awful Alvin the Onion, a tall, thin stalk of a villain with a bulbous head. He peered through a monocle under one of his bushy eyebrows, but noticed the light on behind him.

Awful Alvin turned to his henchman, Lampy, who was...well, a floor lamp. "Turn off your light, Lampy!" said Awful Alvin. "You'll give away our location!"

Lampy didn't respond, so Awful Alvin reached over and switched Lampy's light off himself.

"We can't let Larryboy and Chief Croswell see us now. After all, the test on Angus Mushroom worked perfectly! Soon I shall be able to unleash my *awful* plan! Then Larryboy and all of Bumblyburg will be listening to me and only me! **HA HA HA HA HA HA HA!**"

For some reason, Lampy didn't laugh along.

Half an hour later, Angus's mother, Gladis Mushroom, arrived to take her son home. Angus was waiting with Chief Croswell and Larryboy, who kept jumping around and bumping into walls with a lady's hat still on his head.

"Are you okay, Larryboy?" asked Gladis.

"Of course!" said Larryboy. "Why does everyone keep asking me that?"

Chief Croswell turned to Gladis. "We're glad you're here," he said. "We've been questioning Angus for half an hour, but he won't tell us why he was riding his scooter so recklessly. He just won't listen to us!"

Gladis looked at her son with a frown that let Angus know he was in big trouble. "Why do you look so mad?" asked Angus. "I was only doing what you told me to do."

"What are you talking about?" she said.

"You said, 'Take your scooter and play in traffic!'" said Angus.

"I said no such thing!" said Gladis. "I said, 'Get some sugar for making taffy.'" She turned to Chief Croswell and said, "I love to make taffy! My specialty is chicken-flavored taffy!"

Larryboy, who was still covered in purple gelatin, wearing a life preserver around his tummy and a lady's hat on his head, and still had pants full of jumping beans, tripped and fell into a puddle.

CHAPTER 4

GIVE ME A HOME WHERE THE COCKROACHES ROAM

Before we go any further with our story, we should probably go back and talk about Awful Alvin. You need to know how truly *awful* he is.

Awful Alvin, like any other villain worth his weight in doomsday dungarees, had a secret underground lair. Awful Alvin's particular secret underground lair was a humble, starter lair on the outskirts of Bumblyburg. It was a pretty bad neighborhood, but not quite as awful as Awful Alvin would have liked. Something to work up to, he thought. The roaches and vermin made it feel like home, though, so Awful Alvin had put out his "Unwelcome" mat and settled in.

Second-hand computers and lame lab equipment surrounded him. The kind of stuff you grew tired of

when you were six. Still, by keeping the lights low and
never cleaning, Awful Alvin was able to create a creepy
enough setting for villainy and outdated computer games.

Lights flashed, liquids bubbled, turbines whirred, gen-
erators chugged, and an array of devices blipped and
chirped a language all their own. Not to mention, something behind the refrigerator really stunk!

By Awful Alvin's side stood his faithful partner in
crime, Lampy. During his years of villainy, Awful Alvin
had been so awful that he had driven away all his
friends. Like the time in the tropics when he replaced

Apple

Strudel's sunscreen with olive oil and burned his light and flaky crust. Or the time when he scared the Pumpkin Brothers half to death by filling their beds with fake seeds and orange Silly String while they slept.

After a while, Lampy was the only one who seemed to be able to put up with him.

"Lampy!" said Awful Alvin as they returned to their lair. "The test was a success! The Ear Wacks worked perfectly!"

Awful Alvin held up a small velvet box and opened the lid. He reached in and took out a tiny blinking gadget, no larger than a ladybug. But it wasn't a ladybug. It was an Ear Wack. Taking a ladybug out of the box at this point would make absolutely no sense whatsoever.

"Who would ever think such a small, unnoticeable thing as my Ear Wacks could interfere with something so important as listening?" Alvin pondered.

The first part of his evil plan had worked to perfection when he had slipped the first pair of experimental Ear Wacks into Angus Mushroom's bedroom the night before. He placed the box beside Angus's bed and left a note reading, "Hey, kid! Tired of always having to listen to adults telling you what do? Then try these new Ear Wacks! You'll be able to fool your parents and teachers into thinking that you're listening, when actually, you'll only hear what you *want* to hear!"

This sounded just great to Angus, and he eagerly put the Ear Wacks into his ears. Instantly, he began hearing only what he *wanted* to hear.

When his mom scolded, "Angus! You're late for breakfast," Angus heard, "Angus, you're great for being so fast!"

As he headed out the door for school, his mom called, "Honey, be sure to get some sugar for making taffy!" And, as you already know, what Angus heard was, "Honey, be sure to take your scooter and play in traffic!"

The Ear Wacks had worked perfectly! Not only had Angus heard what he wanted to hear and nothing more, but the Ear Wacks also caused him to ride his scooter recklessly, which caused Larryboy to end up with a lady's hat on his head.

Things couldn't have gone any better if Awful Alvin had planned it that way. Of course, he *had* planned it that way. So, in his final analysis, Awful Alvin had to conclude that things could not have gone any better.

But this was only the beginning. Angus was a small potato (or, more accurately, a small mushroom). Awful Alvin was after the *big* prize now. He was after Larryboy! And when he caught the superhero, Awful Alvin had something *especially* awful planned.

"Behold the Extreme Ear Wacks, Lampy!" From a very large box, Awful Alvin carefully lifted two glowing objects. The softball-sized orbs pulsed orange, like hot metal, and caused a slight tremor in the air.

"When these are placed in the super-suction ears of that purple pretender, Larryboy will have to listen to me, and only ME, for the rest of his days!" Awful Alvin put the Extreme Ear Wacks back in their box and began laughing. **"HA HA HA HA HA!** My plan is so brilliant that if I hadn't come up with it myself, I wouldn't have believed that someone could come up with a plan so brilliant! But I, Awful Alvin, am brilliant! *Awfully* brilliant! So I do believe it! I do! I do! **HA HA HA HA!"**

CHAPTER 5

COFFEE ANYONE?

Later that day, Bob the Tomato sat at his desk, sipping coffee from his "World's Sauciest Editor" mug, and thinking of all the reasons that it was really fun to be editor of the *Daily Bumble* newspaper. "Reason number thirty-six...I can have all the hot coffee I want! Reason number thirty-seven...If I had feet, I could put them up on my desk, and no one would tell me I couldn't! Reason number thirty-eight...I can sit around thinking of useless lists, and it looks like I'm working..."

Just then, Junior Asparagus burst into his office. "Editor Bob!" said Junior.

"Waaaa!" said Bob, as he awoke from his daydreaming. He was so startled by Junior that he knocked over the cup of steaming hot coffee on his desk. "Oh, no! Can somebody get Larry, the janitor, in here?" he yelled. Then, he looked back at Junior. "Junior Asparagus! Haven't I told you never to burst into my office while I'm daydream...um...working!?"

"Well, yeah," said Junior. "But I've got a really great lead on a story! You see Angus Mushroom wasn't listening to his mother and…"

Bob jumped in without listening. "Wait a minute! Since when is it news when a kid doesn't listen to his mother? It happens every day. Why it happens every minute! Right now, somewhere in Bumblyburg, some kid's not listening," Bob continued without letting Junior get a word in edgewise. "I've tried to explain this before, Junior. When a dog bites a person, that's *not* news. It happens every day. When a person bites a dog, *that's* news! It hardly ever happens. Except with my Grandpa Ed and his dog, Rusty. But that's the exception! I'm not going to cover a story about kids not listening. I can't! I hope you understand."

Junior sulked out of Bob's office. He *knew* there was more to this story. He decided that he couldn't give up! He hadn't given up when he was writing stories for the *Bumblyburg Elementary Reader*. His determination allowed him to break the big story on suspiciously shorter recesses. And he had to work hard to get some of his other stories published, such as "Turbocharge Your Gerbil Wheel," the much talked about article that explained how to popularize motor sports with domestic rodents.

Junior decided that this not-listening story had to be covered! He decided right then and there that he would go interview Angus Mushroom…right after school.

Back in his office, Bob the Tomato was getting redder by the minute. He was extremely annoyed that Larry

wasn't in his office yet. He was just about to place an ad for a new janitor when he heard the voice of Gladis Mushroom.

"Yoo hoo!" she said.

"Mrs. Mushroom?" said Bob. "What are you doing here?"

"Well, I just made a batch of my famous chicken-flavored taffy, and I was wondering if you wanted some."

"Well, I..." said Bob just as Larry rushed into the room.

"I got here as soon as I could, Bob!"

"Finally!" Bob groaned.

"What is it, Bob? One of the printing presses needs its thingamabob adjusted? A massive roll of newsprint is off its doohickey? The folding mechanism all cattywumpus?" Larry couldn't wait to actually fix something.

"No, it's coffee," Bob said, pointing to the site of the spill. "That mop should do the trick. Now, while you clean up, I'm gonna go have some taffy!"

CHAPTER 6

SPEAK SOFTLY AND CARRY A BIG MOP

Larry was cleaning up the last of the coffee spill when his mop handle began to vibrate. "I think my mop has had a little too much caffeine," he thought. Then he remembered that his trusted friend and butler, Archie, had installed a digital communications device into the mop handle so he could contact Larryboy when necessary.

"Hello, Master Larry," Archie said. "Can you hear me?"

"Yes, Archie," Larry answered, speaking into the mop handle. But he couldn't find the handy video screen. "You're coming in loud and clear! This thing is so cool. It's the best thing to hit the janitorial world since blue toilet water!"

"Hello? Master Larry, are you there?" Larry could hear Archie, but it was apparent that Archie could not hear Larry.

"Are you talking directly into the mop?" Archie said. "You need to speak directly into it."

Now Larry remembered. He was supposed to turn the mop upside down and talk directly into it. But the bottom of his mop was in the bucket, and the bucket had coffee in it. Larry looked around Bob's office and found a "World's Sauciest Editor" mug and poured the coffee into it.

Then he flipped the bucket and mop over his head and stuck his head into it. "Archie! Can you hear me now?" Larry shouted.

Larry's voice boomed into the headphones that Archie was wearing, causing him to grit his teeth into a distorted grin. "Master Larry," Archie said with a sigh, "take the bucket off your head. It creates quite an echo."

Larry lifted the bucket off his head, which allowed the screen to come into focus. "There you are!"

"Master Larry, I just wanted to remind you about your superhero class tonight at the Bumblyburg Community

College. I'll see you right after class."

"Really? Will you be in the hall when I come out of class?" Larry asked.

"No, I'll be here, at home," Archie replied.

"So technically, you won't see me right after class," Larry said with a frown.

"Technically, no," Archie agreed.

"Because even in good traffic with the Larry-Mobile, I may not get there until…"

"I understand," Archie interrupted. "I'll see you moments after you arrive home."

"Really? Will you be waiting for me at the door?" Larry asked.

"Perhaps you should get back to your janitorial duties, Master Larry," Archie said. "Before you arouse suspicion."

"Oh, right, Archie! Toodles!" Larry said, switching off the mop before he went back to cleaning Bob's office.

CHAPTER 7

THE EAR WACKS UNRAVELS

Junior Asparagus
was a determined reporter. He
always got his story. But this story was
really testing the limits of his patience. He
had been sitting in Angus Mushroom's bedroom
for half an hour, and he wasn't getting *any-
where*! Angus just plain wasn't listening to any of
his questions!

Junior tried again. "What's causing your listening
problem?" he asked for the tenth time.

"I told you," said Angus. "I'm not pausing to do a
whistling album!"

Junior beat his head against his reporter's note-
book. "No, no, no! That's not what I said at all! I've
asked the same question every time! Look, I've even
got it written down right here!" Junior held the note-
book up to Angus and showed him the question.

This time, Angus seemed to understand. "I don't
have a listening problem! But I do have something really cool. It's my new Ear Wacks!"

"EWWW! GROSS!" Junior said, scrunching up his nose. But then, Junior realized something: Angus was having trouble listening, but he could *read* just fine!

"Mom was really mad when I got home," said Angus. "She made me wash my ears out real good. I even had to take my Ear Wacks out! But I put 'em back in when I was done."

Junior winced at the thought of ear wax being yanked out of and put back into someone's ears. He wrote another question on the paper and showed it to Angus.

WHY WOULD YOU WANT TO DO THAT?

"So I can hear what-ever I want to!" Angus said. "It was easy. I just reached in and pulled the Ear Wacks right out! Then I stuck them right back in again."

Junior, normally not squeamish, was getting a little greener around the stalk. But he knew a good report-er didn't let his feelings get in the way, so he wrote another question.

IT CAME OUT IN ONE BIG CHUNK?

"No, it's little," said Angus. "Want to see it?"

Junior nodded nervously, not really wanting to look.

But when Angus showed him the small blinking Ear
Wacks devices, his reporter's instincts took over.

"What are *those*?"

"Ear Wacks!" Angus said again. "Like I've been telling
you all along."

He showed Junior the
box they came in, and
Junior read the note that
came with them: "Hey,
kid! Tired of always hav-
ing to listen to adults tell
you what do? Then try
these new Ear Wacks!
You'll be able to fool your
parents and teachers
into thinking that you're
listening, when actually,
you'll only hear what *you*
want to hear!"

Now Junior understood! Those gizmos were called Ear
Wacks. It wasn't ordinary ear wax that was causing the
listening problem. It was Ear Wacks!

"Where did they come from?" Junior asked, and then
listened as Angus explained that they were right on the
table next to the open window when he woke up that
morning. Someone had planted them there while he slept!

"So you don't hear anything with them in?"

"Only when you don't want to," Angus said, putting

them back in. "You only hear what you *want* to hear!"

Junior stopped to think about what this meant. He thought about all the times that kids didn't want to listen to something important! Directions, rules, guidance, and all sorts of information that came from teachers, parents, doctors...even God! Where would it end?

It would be very tempting to just stop listening to what you didn't want to hear. But the consequences could be disastrous! Junior knew that Ear Wacks were a serious threat to Bumblyburg, and he had to stop them from getting into anyone else's ears.

Junior turned the box over to see if there was anything else written on it. On the bottom, he noticed the initials M.M.

"M.M.!" Junior shouted.

Just then, Gladis Mushroom popped her head in the door. "Anyone want some taffy?"

"You bet!" said Angus. His ears worked just fine when it came to hearing about taffy. But Junior Asparagus knew he had no time for taffy.

"Thanks, Mrs. Mushroom, but I've got to get this down to the *Daily Bumble* right away so I can warn everyone about this mysterious M.M. before he plants any more Ear Wacks!"

Junior rushed out of the room leaving Mrs. Mushroom with a confused expression. "Why would anyone want to plant ear wax?"

CHAPTER 8

AN EAR-REGULAR STORY

Bob the Tomato was heading down the hall on his way back to his office at the *Daily Bumble*. As he walked along, he was daydreaming again. This time, he was thinking about how much fun it would be to play in a pool filled with grape gelatin. You could bounce all over the place, play bouncy bowling, turn somersaults, and…

"Editor Bob!" Junior yelled as he burst into the *Daily Bumble building*.

"Waaaa!" said Bob as he once again broke out of his daydreaming.

Junior rushed up to Bob, "I've got big news! Ear Wacks are what's prevented Angus Mushroom from listening!"

"Ear wax?" Bob replied. **"EEEWWW!** Isn't that a little ear-regular?" He chuckled at his own little joke. "Well, I'm glad we got to the bottom of *that* big story!"

"No, you don't understand," Junior persisted. "It *is* a big story!

We have to warn people before everyone has Ear Wacks!"

"Junior, I think most folks already have ear wax," Bob said with a grin. "I'm afraid that's not a good enough story for the *Daily Bumble*. Now if you'll excuse me, I've got some important daydrea…I mean work to do!"

Bob went back to his office and was pleased to see Larry working. The coffee spill had been cleaned up. *Wow*, he thought, *Larry even brought me a new cup of coffee!* He walked over and took a big gulp from his "World's Sauciest Editor" mug, not knowing that he was about to drink a fresh cup of squeezed mop.

"Something wrong, Bob?" asked Larry. "You're looking a little green…and that's unusual for you."

Bob didn't respond. He was too busy feeling ill.

Larry shrugged and walked out into the hall, where he ran into Junior Asparagus. "What's up, Junior?" he asked.

"I've got to think of a way to convince Bob that there's a serious threat to Bumblyburg!" Junior insisted. "And I'm not talking about the return of polyester."

"Um…Bob doesn't seem to be talking to anyone just now," Larry said. "Why don't you tell me about it?"

"It's right here in this box," Junior said, taking out the small box labeled "Ear Wacks." "It's the Ear Wacks that came out of Angus Mushroom's ears."

"EEEWWW!" Larry said, wrinkling his nose.

"No, look!" Junior said, opening the box.

"EEEWWW! EAR WAX!" Larry said, wrinkling his entire face and hiding behind his mop. Then he peeked

ility to listen," Archie said. "And according to the omputer, the initials 'M.M.' seem to stand for Masked essenger."

"Aha! Then it's *not* Moses Malone!"

"No. I'm afraid you'll have to look elsewhere for this asked Messenger."

"He could be hard to spot. He might be wearing a ask," Larryboy said.

"Correct. That means he could even be in your class pos-g as a superhero," Archie pointed out. "Be on your toes, aster Larry!"

Larryboy looked down, a little confused about how he uld do that. "Wow! A villain in superhero class! Wait until ell the other superheroes! They'll be so excited!"

around the mop strands and saw the two blinking dots, like electronic ladybugs. "Ooooo! That's pretty cool!"

For the next five minutes, Larry listened with rapt attention as Junior told him what he had learned about the Ear Wacks and the M.M. initials. He told Larry how important it was to warn everyone before the Ear Wacks got out to the general public.

"This sounds like a job for Larryboy!" Larry said, striking a heroic pose.

"Yeah!" Junior said, smiling at the janitor's sudden goofiness. "Someone should tell him!"

"I am that *someone*!" Larry said. Now he was thinking like Larryboy! This had to be the work of one of his arch-enemies. But he couldn't think of anyone with the initials M.M., other than former NBA star, Moses Malone. Larry was pretty sure it wasn't him. He knew he had to get a pair of Ear Wacks to Archie for analysis.

"Could I have those?" Larry asked Junior, taking the Ear Wacks. "I have some equipment in my janitor's closet that could give us some answers. You'd be surprised what I can do with a good plunger and some duct tape. Don't worry, Junior. I'll take it from here."

Junior reluctantly agreed. "Okay, but if your equipment doesn't work, be sure to get it in the hands of Larryboy!"

"Will do!" Larry shouted as he disappeared around the corner.

CHAPTER 9

A CLASS ACT

After Larryboy got
the Ear Wacks to Archie, he v
to his superhero class at the Bun
Community College. The classroom v
with a colorful assortment of costumes
cealed the true identities of the superh
Just as Bok Choy, the teacher of the clas
his way to the front of classroom, Larryboy
buckle began beeping. All of the superheroes
their belts to see if their belt radios were beepir

"Mine!" Larry said as he got up to step out in
hall. "Sorry, for the interruption fellas, but I'm gon
to take this. Superhero stuff, ya know."

"Yo! Larryboy speaking."

"Master Larry, it's Archie."

"Well, of course it's you, Archie. Nobody else
number," Larry said.

"I've determined that the Ear Wacks have
microchip that somehow interferes with the

"No, Master Larry!" Archie said. "You can't let the Masked Messenger know you're on to him. Say nothing to anyone!"

There was no response. Archie waited a moment until he realized that Larryboy was taking his advice a little too literally. "I mean say nothing to anyone in *class*," Archie clarified.

"Oh," said Larryboy.

Bok Choy was already speaking as Larryboy returned to the classroom. "So if you'll turn in your *Superhero Handbook* to Section 20, Paragraph 1, Line 5, we come to today's lesson: 'Let the wise listen and add to their learning, and let the discerning get guidance.'"

Larryboy stood in the doorway and scanned the classroom looking at the masks the superheroes were wearing. "Could one of them be the Masked Messenger?" he whispered to himself.

"Electro-Melon, could you tell us why listening is so important?" Bok Choy asked.

"Certainly! Even though we're all superheroes with super gadgets and super powers, we don't know everything there is to know," he said. "We can always learn from someone else, whether they're young or old."

"That's right, EM. Very good," Bok Choy said. "Everyone

can teach us something."

Larryboy continued looking around the class and found something very disturbing: There was not just one superhero with the letters M.M. on his mask... there were two! Oh no!

Bok Choy continued the lesson. "The second part of that message is to let the discerning get guidance. That means we also need to be careful to whom we listen. Raisinboy, would you care to elaborate on that?"

"Yes sir! That means it's important to listen to those who want what's best for us. People like our parents, our teachers, and God, to name a few."

"Good answer, Raisinboy. It's also important that we can trust the people to whom we listen."

CHAPTER 10

LOOKING FOR M. AND M. AND GOING PLAIN NUTS

Larryboy was worried. How would he ever be able to figure out which superhero with an M.M. on their mask was the real Masked Marvel? He'd have to talk to them, but how could he do that with Bok Choy in the room? Bok Choy would probably catch him talking, and Larryboy didn't want to have to go stand in the corner again. That dunce hat really clashed with his costume!

Suddenly, Larryboy had an idea. He'd distract Bok Choy and get him out of the room. Then he could weed out the real villain.

Larryboy burst into the room, pretending to be in great distress. "Bok Choy! Bok Choy!" he cried. "There's a terrible emergency! Some superhero must act!"

All the superheroes sprang to their feet, ready for action.

"Um…no," said Larryboy. "Only Bok Choy can handle *this* emergency!"

"Why is that?" asked

Bok Choy. "There are plenty of capable superheroes here."

"Well, uh...um...I mean...oh! This emergency is taking place in the *teacher's lounge*! Only teachers are allowed in there! And...they're out of coffee!"

"Jumpin' Java!" shouted Bok Choy. "This is a caffeine catastrophe! You superheroes stay here! I'll take care of this!"

Bok Choy leaped onto his desk, struck a heroic pose, and uttered his personal heroic cry, "Bok-Bok-Bok-Bok-Bok Choy, away!" He then rushed from the room.

As soon as Bok Choy exited, Larryboy slid up to the first of the superheroes with an M.M. on his mask.

"Nice mask!" Larryboy said. "I'm Larryboy, the superhero right here in Bumblyburg. And you are?"

"Muskie Melon," said the superhero with M.M. on his mask.

"Oh, that explains the smell," Larryboy said, disappointed that he wasn't the Masked Messenger.

"Sorry, I'm a little ripe," Muskie explained. "I didn't have a chance to shower after my Tie-Bow class."

"Tie-Bow class?" Larryboy inquired.

"Yeah, some of us superheroes who wear capes were having trouble keeping them tied when we were chasing after villains," Muskie explained. "We learned some new bows that won't come undone as easily. And we also looked at some fascinating..."

"Yeah, yeah," said Larryboy. "Good to meet you. Gotta go."

Well, one down. That meant that the other hero must be the real villain.

CHAPTER 11

WHEN WELL-MEANING SUPERHEROES ATTACK

Larryboy quickly moved
to another desk that was beside the
other superhero with M.M. on her mask.
"Nifty mask," Larryboy said. "Is it new?"
"As a matter of fact, it is," she said. "My old
one was a poly-blend and gave me a horrible
rash, when I got hot chasing villains. This one is
high-tech Cottonesque. Wicks away the perspiration."
"I get the *message*," Larryboy said with a wink,
trying to trick his new prime suspect.
"Funny you should mention that," the unknown
superhero replied. "I'm very good with messages."
"I bet you are," Larryboy said, standing slowly.
"Well, here's a message from Larryboy! It's not nice to
mess with the ears of Bumblyburg!" With that,
Larryboy shot both of his super-suction ears at the
masked potato! When the other superheroes heard
the commotion, they instinctively activated all of
their super-gadgets.
In a split second, the room was filled with

ropes, grappling hooks, nets, hoses, smoke, bungee cords, squid ink, foam, slingshots, boomerangs, and a saxophone.

Just then, Bok Choy re-entered the room. "Larryboy, there's plenty of coffee in the…" Then he saw the mess. "What's going on here?"

Larryboy spoke up. "I discovered a super-villian infiltrating our class! The Masked Messenger! Her evil plan was to interfere with the ability of our fine citizens to be good lis-

teners, thereby creating chaos and confusion!"

The potato was struggling to say something, but there was a super-suction ear covering her mouth.

"Let's not jump to conclusions," Bok Choy said. "We'll listen to what she has to say before you try to whip her into shape. Release the plungers!"

Larryboy released her, and the potato readjusted her mask. "I should have stayed in Boise where they understand

us spuds," she said. "I am not the Masked Messenger! I am the Mashed Marvel!"

The other superheroes gasped.

"When I said I was good with messages," she continued, "I meant that I'm good with *mental* messages. I can read minds with my super powers."

Yeah, I just bet you can, Larryboy thought.

"No, I really can," the Mashed Marvel replied. "If you would have been a *good listener*, Larryboy, none of this would have happened!"

The other superheroes nodded in agreement as they gathered their super-gadgets and Superhero Handbooks.

"I think we all learned a valuable lesson tonight," said Bok Choy. "Now let's go out and be good listeners! Class dismissed!"

CHAPTER 12

THE STENCHMAN AND HIS HENCHMAN

Larryboy sat at his desk. He felt horrible. He had caused all kinds of trouble by not being a good listener. Worst of all, he had lost the respect of his fellow superheroes.

"Chin up, Larryboy."

It was Awful Alvin the Onion. He had been in the class all along, disguised as Marineboy! Now he and Larryboy were the only ones left in the classroom. Most of the lights were off, except for a floor lamp sitting off to one side.

"So you had a tough night. It happens to all of us," said the disguised onion. "I'm sure the other superheroes will forget all about this...in 10 or 20 years."

"I feel so foolish," Larryboy said. "I wish I was a better listener!"

Awful Alvin had to suppress a giggle. Larryboy was walking right into his trap! "I have just the thing for that," Awful Alvin said, feeling especially awful. "I made these devices specifically to help people listen."

Being careful to stand behind Larryboy, he reached into a large box on the floor and carefully lifted two glowing orbs—the Extreme Ear Wacks! "Just tilt your head back," he said to Larryboy. "You'll be a better listener in no time!"

Awful Alvin needed a little more light to make sure the Extreme Ear Wacks were placed securely. He reached over and pulled Lampy from his strategic position near the wall. Larryboy glanced up as the lamp came into view.

"Oh, hi, Lampy!" he said.

Larryboy's eyes went wide. "Lampy?"

But before he could react, Awful Alvin had attached the Extreme Ear Wacks to Larryboy's super suction ears.

Larryboy heard the squeal of high-pitched tones, like a

radio dial being tuned to a distant station. Now Larryboy saw the villain remove the stolen mask and costume he had been wearing. It was Awful Alvin.

"So, we meet again," said Awful Alvin.

"You ever hear of breath mints?" Larryboy asked the onion-scented villain. But he couldn't even hear his own words! Then, when the static and squealing stopped, he could only hear the sound of Awful Alvin's voice. "Now, Larryboy, you will hear only what *I* want you to hear! And you will ignore hearing all that is good," he snickered. "I may even have you sing the Awful Alvin theme song that I just finished. And it's not as awful as you might suspect!

"I thought you might be onto my plan," Awful Alvin explained. So I put the letters M.M. on the box to throw you off the trail."

Larryboy tried hard not to listen to Awful Alvin's words, even going so far as to try and figure out the words to the Awful Alvin theme song.

MORE THAN JUST AN ONION, HE'S A SUPER ONION SNEAK. HE'S A REALLY ROTTEN STINKER, SO YOU DON'T DANCE CHEEK TO CHEEK.

It was no use! The villain's words took over, and they were the only thing Larryboy could hear. He had to fight it. He had to think of a way to contact Archie and stop this heartless onion!

But how?

CHAPTER 13

OH, WHERE IS MY LARRYBOY?

The next morning, Archie was beside himself with worry. Larry's jammies were neatly folded, his bunny slipper was next to his bed, and his hairbrush was right there in plain sight. It was clear that Larry had not come home after superhero class last night.

Archie got no answer on any of Larryboy's communication devices—not his Mop Video-Phone, not his Belt-Buckle Radio, not his Transistor-Toaster Pastry, and not even on his Digital Toothpick. Archie feared that Larryboy was in the clutches of the Masked Messenger! He called Bok Choy at the Bumblyburg Community College and listened as the professor told him all about the unfortunate incident that happened during superhero class. "So is it possible Larryboy could just be too embarrassed to come home?" Archie asked.

"That could be," Bok Choy said. "But at least he had someone to talk to. When I left, he was with the superhero from Bumbly Bay, Marineboy!"

Archie thanked Bok Choy and turned his attention to the police scanner for possible news of Larryboy's whereabouts.

"Bumblyburg Station, this is car 54."

"Car 54, where are you?"

"We're on the outskirts of Bumblyburg in the Villain's Lair district. We just picked up this avocado we found wandering around here. You're not going to believe this, but guacamole here claims to be a kidnapped superhero from Bumbly Bay. He won't reveal his superhero identity, but he says his costume was stolen by Awful Alvin the Onion."

At that point, Archie put it all together: Larryboy was seen last with Marineboy, who is from Bumbly Bay. Then a superhero from Bumbly Bay claimed Awful Alvin had stolen his costume. Awful Alvin must have been posing as Marineboy when Bok Choy last saw Larryboy!

"Great galloping galoshes!" said Archie. "Larryboy must have fallen into the *awful* clutches of Awful Alvin the Onion…and Lampy."

Meanwhile, in the skies above Bumblyburg, an onion-shaped blimp positioned itself over the Veggie Valley Elementary School. In the blimp's gondola were Awful Alvin, Lampy, Larryboy, and hundreds of small velvet boxes rigged with tiny, tear-shaped parachutes.

Normally, Larryboy would have been uncomfortable at this height. And by "uncomfortable," I mean downright loopy with fear. Normally, he would have been curled up on the floor, calling out for his rubber duckie. But this was not a normal time for Larryboy. He was not acting like himself. He was acting less like a superhero and more like an un-superhero. His eyes were half-closed, and his mind could only register the constant villainous cackling of Awful Alvin.

"Prepare to watch the beginning of the end of the beginning that ends the begin … well, just watch!" said Awful Alvin. "Each of these precious parachutes will carry a pair of Ear Wacks to the unsuspecting playground below."

When the kids at Veggie Valley place the Ear Wacks in their ears, Awful Alvin knew they would only be able to hear one thing…his own hideous commands! The kids would become his drones, just like Larryboy…except without plunger ears.

"We are over the drop site!" Awful Alvin announced. "Lampy! Release the Ear Wacks!"

Lampy stood straight and remained very still.

"This is no time for second thoughts, Lampy. Ear Wacks away!"

Lampy's shade moved slightly in the breeze, but the trap door beneath the boxes remained closed. "You're right, Lampy," he said. "Maybe we should let our special guest have the honor. Larryboy! Pull the lever and drop the Ear Wacks down to the school children of Veggie Valley!"

Under the control of the Extreme Ear Wacks and Awful Alvin's villainous voice, Larryboy pulled the lever and released the Ear Wacks to fall to the children of Veggie Valley Elementary School.

CHAPTER 14

THE EAR WAX UNRAVELS

Back at the Larry-Cave, Archie paced nervously back and forth. Suddenly, the Larry-Alarm went off! The Larry-Radar had detected an unknown object in the skies above Bumblyburg!

"To the Larry-Scope" yelled Archie.

Archie blushed, as he realized there was no one there other than Larry's rubber duckie. He was talking to himself again.

Archie regained his composure and pressed a button, which caused a high-power telescope to emerge from one of the turrets on the mansion. It was a clear day, and it didn't take long to spot the slow-moving, onion-shaped blimp in the sky over Bumblyburg.

Archie zoomed in on the blimp. "Oh my, Master Larry," Archie said as he saw Larryboy standing next to Awful Alvin. "What has he done to you?" Then, Archie noticed Larryboy's glassy-eyed stare and the glowing orbs in his ears. He zoomed in on the orbs with full magnification. He could make out

several small words. **"IF...YOU...CAN...READ...THIS, ... YOU... HAVE...A...REALLY...GOOD...TELESCOPE!"**

Then he pulled back a little on the zoom function and read the larger letters: "Extreme Ear Wacks."

Ear Wacks! Suddenly, Archie realized why Larryboy hadn't been responding on his communicator. He was under the control of the Ear Wacks.

"This is terrible!" said Archie. "Those Ear Wacks are extremely powerful! If I don't find a way to neutralize them quickly, the damage could become permanent!"

Archie took the smaller set of Ear Wacks that Larryboy had given him down to the Larry-Lab. He had to study them to find a way to disarm the Ear Wacks! The future of Bumblyburg was at stake!

Meanwhile, back at Veggie Valley Elementary, Awful

Alvin's plan was working perfectly. Junior Asparagus was running around trying to warn his classmates not to put the Ear Wacks in their ears. But none of them were listening. The kids were excited at the prospect of only hearing what they wanted to hear.

But instead of hearing only what they wanted to hear, the kids ended up hearing something no one wanted to hear: The *awful* voice of Awful Alvin! They became unwilling servants, just like Larryboy. The kids surrounded Junior, and soon, even he had Ear Wacks in his ears.

Alvin's blimp landed on the playground. "Touch down!" he said. "Seven points for us, Lampy! Or is it six? What does it matter? I make the rules now, and I say it's seven! Let's get some cheerleaders. Maybe a mascot, too. An onion ring might be nice. Go rings! It has a nice 'ring' to it, don't you think, Lampy? **HA HA HA HA!**"

Normally, Larryboy would have taken Awful Alvin to jail just for making such a bad pun. But all he could do now was listen through the Extreme Ear Wacks.

"Okay, my faithful kiddie brigade," Awful Alvin said to the Ear-Wacked children of Veggie Valley Elementary. "It's time for you to do my bidding! And I bid that you shall do *awful* things that will please me, and only me!"

Then Awful Alvin looked at Larryboy and explained how the children of Bumblyburg were now under *his* control. "I've taken away the authority of anyone they've ever listened to...parents, teachers, police officers...even God! They are all powerless in the eyes...I mean ears...of the children! **HA HA HA HA!**" he cackled.

He had the kids line up and started giving them awful commands that only Awful Alvin's awful mind could ever have come up with. First, he commanded them to stand on their heads. Then he commanded them to hop around like kangaroos. After that, he commanded them to scratch that spot on his back that he could never reach.

Then, he commanded them to do something so awful that it was almost *too awful* for even Awful Alvin. He commanded them to...*country line dance!*

Larryboy and the Veggie Valley kids could only helplessly obey each of the commands.

CHAPTER 15

ARCHIE MAKES AN EERIE, WACKY DISCOVERY

Meanwhile, back at the Larry-Cave, Archie was working feverishly to find a way to disable the Ear Wacks, but nothing was working. Picking up a tiny Ear Wack, Archie carried it over to the electron microscope, passing near the communications console.

As he did, an ear-piercing screech echoed through the Larry-Cave. In the gondola of the blimp, Larryboy heard the same screech, only louder! Awful Alvin heard it, too, EVEN LOUDER, due to the microchips implanted in his inner ears.

"OWWW!" Archie shrieked in the Larry-Cave.

"YOUCH!!" Larryboy yelped in the blimp's gondola.

"OUCHIE-WAWAAAAA!!!" Awful Alvin screamed.

Achie flipped off the microphone switch, and everything went silent. "I must have left the microphone on when I last attempted to call Master Larry," he mumbled to himself. "That screech was audio feedback from the microphone."

Archie had accidentally discovered a way to communi-
cate to the Ear Wacks! With some extra fine-tuning, maybe
he could reach Larryboy. But how could he counter the effect
of the Extreme Ear Wacks?

That part would have to be up to Larryboy. Only Larryboy
could listen and learn by stopping to think about what he
was hearing and from whom. He would have to discern
whom he trusted and who was telling him what was best
for him. And that certainly wasn't Awful Alvin.

When the ringing in his ears subsided, Larryboy thought
he'd heard Archie's distinctive voice. It sounded like he had
said, **"OWWW!"**

To Awful Alvin, it had sounded like the ringing of
a thousand bells—a thousand bells that went 'Owww.'
When he could hear again at last, he said, "Lampy! Shed
some light on this problem! What caused that malfunc-
tion? I want some answers *now*!"

CHAPTER 16

THE EVIL HAS LANDED

Lampy provided no answers. But he didn't claim there was any further threat, either. So long as the Veggie kids continued to follow Alvin's orders, everything seemed to be going according to plans.

"No one can stop me now!" Awful Alvin screeched. "Now Larryboy will be using his super-powers to help me do any awful thing I choose—like taking cuts in lines at the movies, checking out with more than ten items in the express lane, driving alone in the car pool lane, swimming without a life guard at the community pool, and tearing off those "Do Not Remove" labels on mattresses. The list is endless!"

Picking up his Ear Wacks transmitter, Awful Alvin announced, "Children of Bumblyburg! It's time for more of your Awful Assignments. The reign of Awful Alvin the Onion is about to begin! **HA HA HA HA HA HA!**"

The villain's maniacal laugh was still ringing in Larryboy's ears when he once again heard high-pitched squeals. Suddenly, Awful Alvin's voice seemed to be mixing with Archie's. If there was ever a time Larryboy needed guidance, it was now!

Larryboy thought back to the lesson he'd heard in his superhero class. He realized he had been listening in class, but he hadn't really paid attention. He thought hard. *Let the wise…something…and get guidance. Or was it guide the wise to avoid something … ? Maybe "Get the rice pudding if you have a yearning." That doesn't seem right either.*

Larryboy focused all his concentration on the lesson, and finally, not only the words came to him, but the meaning! "Let the wise listen and add to their learning, and let the discerning get guidance."

He just had to listen to the people he trusted, those who loved him and wanted what was best for him. Suddenly, it became perfectly clear and he could hear only Archie!

"Master Larry," Archie said quietly. "If you truly learned your lesson, you should be able to hear me. I have a plan. Now, listen carefully."

Archie went through the plan with Larryboy, who carefully listened to the guidance from his trusted butler and mentor. The superhero knew it was his only chance to defeat Awful Alvin and save Bumblyburg. He had to break the spell of the Ear Wacks once and for all!

CHAPTER 17

EVIL ON THE INSIDE, CHEWY ON THE OUTSIDE

Grabbing a list of student names he had stolen from Veggie Valley Elementary School, Awful Alvin began giving out awful assignments. "Percy Pea! You're going to be in charge of putting 'Wet Paint' signs on all benches, bushes, doors, sidewalks, trees, and streets. Okay. Hop to it." Percy nodded and moved to obey.

"Laura Carrot!" he called. "You will be in charge of mixing the recyclables with the regular garbage. Go on, now."

Awful Alvin continued giving out Awful Assignments to all the kids—drinking directly out of milk cartons at the grocery store, replacing #2 pencils with #3's, breaking the bottom tips off pointed ice cream cones, losing the caps to colored markers—until only Junior Asparagus remained.

"Ah, Junior Asparagus, my little green friend. I have an *especially* awful job for you," cackled Awful Alvin.

Junior snapped to action, but instead of listening to Awful Alvin, he concentrated on what he had heard from his mom and dad. They had taught him to listen only to the people who loved him—the people he could trust. This was his chance to help Larryboy! "I won't listen to you, Mr. Awful! I'm only going to listen to the people who care about me. You care about me, don't you Larryboy?"

Junior's words got through to Larryboy loud and clear.

"I sure do, Junior! Bumblyburg is in need of a hero, and **I AM THAT HERO!**"

Taking aim at Awful Alvin, he fired both super-suction ears in rapid succession. Unfortunately, they fell to the ground and bounced at the villain's feet. "Uh-oh," Larryboy said.

"Did you really think I wouldn't deactivate your firing mechanism?" Awful Alvin asked. "Please, Larryboy. Give me a little more credit than that."

"Well, I have plenty of other weapons to use against you!" Larryboy said. "Don't I, Archie? Oh, I forgot he can't hear me unless I turn this on."

Larryboy activated his Belt Buckle radio and a tremendous screech of feedback filled the air. Luckily for Larryboy, the Extreme Ear Wacks no longer had any effect.

Unluckily for Awful Alvin, his inner-ear implants were still cranked to the max. He clutched his ears in pain, but he managed to get out one command.

"Children, seize him! Switch off his Belt Buckle radio!" he cried. The kids dutifully surrounded Larryboy!

"No, wait!" the superhero protested. "Kids, it's me, Larryboy! Listen to me. Don't you trust me? You know I want what's best for all of you! You have to choose very carefully when you decide to whom you will listen. I'm the good guy. He's the bad guy, and he doesn't want to do what's right!"

As Junior switched off Larryboy's Belt Buckle radio, he looked up at his hero and realized that he trusted Larryboy. Larryboy loved him and wanted what was best for him. Awful Alvin did not!

As Junior understood the value of listening to the right people, he was able to shake his head hard enough to cause the Ear Wacks to fall out! He smiled at Larryboy and looked around at the other kids. Percy Pea grinned as he too listened to Larryboy. Then Laura Carrot smiled as the superhero's words came through loud and clear.

Two by two, the Ear Wacks were shaken out of the kids' ears, and everybody realized just how awful Awful Alvin was. As the villain slowly recovered from his latest bout with the screeching feedback, Larryboy quickly hatched a plan.

"Does everyone have chewing gum?" he whispered to the kids. The kids took an assortment of gum from their pockets: Squiggly's Spearmint, Palooka Pop, Molar Madness, Chewy Kablooey, Gooeylicious, Jaw Mashers, Tooth Tinglers.

Every kind of gum imaginable!

"Get chewing!" Larryboy said quietly, as Awful Alvin struggled back to a standing position. "When you get a good, sticky wad, take out your Ear Wacks, stick 'em in the gum, and stick the gum to Awful Alvin."

Everyone started chewing frantically, including Larryboy, who gobbled a whole pack of his favorite grape gum, Bubblyburst.

Awful Alvin's head was still throbbing as he turned to the kids.

"Listen up, children!" he commanded. "Okay, I tricked you into wearing the Ear Wacks. But that doesn't mean you still can't listen to me. In fact, if you listen to me now, you will get to help me mess up the entire school! Doesn't that sound like fun? No more school?"

The kids paused. Messing up the school did sound like fun. But before the kids could do anything, Junior said, "Larryboy's right! Awful Alvin is a bad guy! If we listen to him, we'll end up doing bad stuff, too! We need to listen to those who care about us! Those who care about doing what's right...like Larryboy!"

Junior Asparagus smiled at Larryboy, and Larryboy smiled right back.

Awful Alvin, however, did not smile. Especially when a glistening hunk of pink Palooka Pop hit him squarely on the forehead and stuck tight.

"Who threw that?" Awful Alvin demanded, as a bluish wad of Molar Madness hit his cheek and three other soggy pieces of assorted chewing gum landed on his head. "Lampy! Help me!" the villain cried. But even his faithful friend seemed not to hear.

The kids were determined to bring this villain down by attacking him with colored wads of gum, each with tiny, blinking Ear Wacks inside.

"Stop it! Stop it right now!" Alvin said, slowly realizing deep down in his stinky layers that the Ear Wacks weren't working anymore. He backed away slowly, grabbing Lampy and looking for an escape route.

As Awful Alvin tried to run to his blimp to get away, Larryboy stuck two extremely large wads of purple gum on either side of the villain's head. Two orb-shaped wads of gum glowed and caused a slight tremor in the air.

The Extreme Ear Wacks were no longer in Larryboy's

super-suction ears. They were embedded in the grape gum stuck to Awful Alvin's head, along with hundreds of smaller Ear Wacks stuck all over him.

"I have a little feedback for you, Awful Alvin," Larryboy said. "First of all, don't mess with Bumblyburg. Second of all…this."

Larryboy reached down and switched on his Belt Buckle radio. In that very instant, an onion-splitting pitch of feedback emitted from hundreds of Ear Wacks, plus the Extreme Ear Wacks from Larryboy, launching Awful Alvin and Lampy high into the air over Bumblyburg!

A billowing trail of steam followed Alvin and Lampy as they landed with a splash in the community swimming pool.

"Anyone for onion dip?" Larryboy quipped as the citizens of Bumblyburg cheered!

CHAPTER 18

THERE'S NO TASTE LIKE LIVER AND NO PLACE LIKE HOME

"It's good to be home, Archie," Larry said as he relaxed in his favorite easy chair. "And it's good to have Bumblyburg back to normal."

"Indeed it is," said Archie.

"I sure did learn a valuable lesson about listening," Larry said.

"That's good news!" said Archie. "Because I was just going to tell you that it is time for you to get back to your janitor job."

Suddenly, a glassy look came over Larry's eyes. "What was that, Archie? I can't *hear* you. Those Ear Wacks must be affecting me again!"

Archie put a big piece of chewing gum into his mouth and began to chew. "Master Larry," he said. "I have a big wad of Bubblyburst, and I'm not afraid to use it!"

Larry hopped up out of his chair. "Heh heh. I was just kidding! Just *kidding*!" he said as he grabbed his mop and rushed off to work.

LARRYBOY

AND THE SINISTER SNOW DAY

WRITTEN BY
SEAN GAFFNEY

ILLUSTRATED BY
MICHAEL MOORE

BASED ON THE HIT VIDEO SERIES: LARRYBOY
CREATED BY PHIL VISCHER
SERIES ADAPTED BY TOM BANCROFT

ZONDERVAN.com/
AUTHORTRACKER
follow your favorite authors

TABLE OF CONTENTS

CHAPTER 1

BUMBLING IN THE BUMBLE BASEMENT

It was very dark. In fact, it was impossible to see anything at all.

"Ouch!" cried a voice.

"Who's there?" asked a second, squeaky voice.

"It's me," replied the first voice. "Who said, 'Who's there?'"

"I did," said the second voice, getting squeakier.

"What are *you* doing here?" demanded the first voice.

"What are *you* doing here?" squeaked the second.

"I asked first," the first voice insisted. "Ouch, I stepped on something hard!"

"That's me!" the second voice squeaked in pain.

"What's going on here?" cried Bob, as suddenly the lights were turned on.

Bob, the editor of the *Daily Bumble*, stood near the light switch of the newspaper's printing room. Herbert and Wally looked up from the middle of the room where they were standing next to the large printing press. They both looked sheepish.

"What did you find, boss?" asked Vicki, the

Bumble's photographer. She bounded into the room behind Bob. Just then Larry, the newspaper's janitor, peeked into the room, too.

"What's going on?" asked Larry.

"Bob heard intruders in the print room," answered Vicki.

"Intruders!" Larry exclaimed. "This is a job for...excuse me, please."

Larry turned and dashed away. Bob and Vicki watched the janitor for a moment and then looked at each other and shrugged. Larry often acted strangely, and they were becoming used to it. They turned their attention back to Herbert and Wally.

"What are you two doing in my printing-press room?" asked Bob.

"Well..." said Wally.

"Well, what?" demanded Bob.

"I was going to change the headline for tomorrow's sports page," confessed Wally.

"Change it?" asked Bob. "What's wrong with 'Bumbly-burg Baseball Has Bats in Its Belfry'?"

"Nothing," said Wally. "I just thought a better headline might say, 'Wally Beats Herbert in Bowling' instead."

"Now why didn't we think of that," sighed Vicki, rolling her eyes.

"What about you?" Bob asked Herbert.

"I was going to change the headline to read, 'Wally Snores,'" said Herbert.

Bob sighed. "When are the two of you ever going to learn?"

"What do you mean?" asked Wally. "We already graduated from school."

"I got straight A's in finger painting," said Herbert. "And that's not easy for a vegetable with no fingers."

"That's not what I mean," said Bob. "You keep letting your petty squabbles get you into trouble."

"What's a 'squabble'?" asked Herbert.

"It's a board game," replied Wally.

"That's Scrabble," said Vicki.

"Oh," said Wally.

"Have no fear, Larryboy is here!" said a voice from the doorway.

Bob, Vicki, Herbert, and Wally turned toward the door and saw...

CHAPTER 2

LARRYBOY TO THE RESCUE!

Larryboy! Supercucumber champion among vegetables, the green guardian of Bumblyburg, and an all-around nice guy!

"Step aside, Bob. I'll take care of these intimidating intruders," announced Larryboy.

"I don't think that will be necessary," said Bob. "These two are..."

But before Bob could finish his sentence, Larryboy leaped over and pushed him aside. Bob stumbled into the control panel of the printing press, and the machine roared to life.

"Don't try to run!" Larryboy yelled at the motionless Herbert and Wally.

"Okay," said Wally. Herbert just nodded.

"Villains always try to run," Larryboy whispered to Vicki. "But I'm too smart for that. Watch!"

POP! Larryboy shot off one of his plunger ears. The suction cup whizzed past the two intruders and wedged into the printing press.

"Hmm," mused Larryboy. "If they had been running, that shot

would have been a direct hit."

"But they aren't running," Vicki noted.

"Really?" asked Larryboy. "Hey, cut that out!"

"Cut what out?" asked Vicki.

"Someone's pulling on my plunger ear," said Larryboy.

Vicki looked at Bob, who looked at Wally, who looked at Herbert. No one was pulling either of Larryboy's plunger ears.

"No one is pulling either of your plunger ears," said Vicki. "But look at the printing press!"

Everyone looked at the spot where Larryboy's ear hit the machine. The plunger ear was being pulled inside the press, dragging Larryboy along with it!

"Help!" shouted Larryboy frantically, as he was being pulled closer to the press.

"Turn the machine off!" shouted Vicki. Larryboy was getting closer still.

"I'm trying!" shouted Bob. Larryboy was now pressed against the machine.

"Too late!" shouted Wally, as Larryboy disappeared into the press.

"I want to shout something too!" shouted Herbert, feeling left out.

It was indeed too late. Larryboy had been pulled into the printing press. Bob, Vicki, Herbert, and Wally looked on helplessly. The machine groaned.

"Ouch," winced Bob. "That's *got* to hurt."

CLANK! CLUNK! SPLAT! The machine continued making odd noises.

"Look, he's up there!" Wally exclaimed.

Larryboy briefly appeared near the top of the printing press.

"I'm OK," Larryboy said, before being pulled back into the machine.

"Yes, but is the printing press OK?" asked Bob. As if in answer, ink began spurting out the sides of the press.

"Oh, no," moaned Bob.

CLANK! CLUNK! SPLAT! And then suddenly a final **SPLOOSH!** Larryboy shot out of the end of the machine. He was bundled with a stack of newspapers, and the head-line "School Back in Session" was printed across his fore-head.

"Are you all right?" asked Vicki.

"Sure," said Larryboy. He was acting tough to impress Vicki.

"That's one way to get your uniform pressed," she joked.

"Now we're going to have to reset the whole thing," said Bob. "It's going to be a late night."

"Sorry," said Larryboy.

"Don't feel sorry for us," said Vicki. "You should feel sorry for Larry, our janitor."

"Meeee?" squealed Larryboy. "I mean, *me* feel sorry for Larry? Why should I feel sorry for Larry?"

"Look at this place," said Vicki. The room was a mess. Ink was splattered everywhere—on the walls, on the ceiling, even on Bob. "It's going to take Larry days to clean up this room."

"Ulp," said Larryboy.

"Come on, Vicki," said Bob. "We have a paper to put out."

CHAPTER 3

WHETHER THE WEATHER IS SUNNY OR NOT

WHAP!

A newspaper bounced against the door of the Asparagus' house. The door flew open as Junior dashed out, snatched up the paper, and ran back inside. He raced to the living room, plopped down on the floor, and opened it up. Junior quickly flipped past the book review of Chief Croswell's best-seller, *Littering, Loitering, and the Law*. He barely saw the photo of Herbert and Wally breaking the world eating record as they devoured a sixty-foot-tall leaning tower of pizza. He found the page he was looking for and eagerly scanned it.

"Rats!" Junior grumbled, as his dad came around the corner.

"What's wrong, Son?" he asked.

"It's the weather report," said Junior. "I was hoping for a snowstorm this morning."

"A snowstorm in *September*?" Junior's dad chuckled. "That would be surprising. But don't worry. It will snow in a couple of months."

"A couple of months?" Junior yelped. "But

that's a lifetime away! I want it to snow today."

"But if it snowed today," his dad reasoned, "they might have to cancel school. You wouldn't want that, would you?"

Junior's dad had missed the point completely. That is exactly why Junior wanted it to snow!

"Dad," said Junior, "you completely missed the point. That is exactly why I want it to snow!"

"I thought you liked school," he said.

"Sure, when I was a *kid*," said Junior. "But now that I'm growing up, I have better things to do."

"Growing up? But you *are* still in grade school," said Dad.

"The way I see it," said Junior, "counting preschool, I've already had several years of classes. So I'm basically nearing adulthood!"

Dad chuckled and picked the paper up from the floor. "Really?" he said. "Well, just remember that God wants everyone to keep learning. Even grown-ups! When you stop learning, you stop growing."

"Sure, Dad," Junior said. "Can I look at the paper again?"

"Of course. What are you looking for?"

"I forgot to see if it's going to snow *tomorrow*," said Junior.

"It's not going to snow tomorrow," his dad replied.

"Too bad," moaned Junior, as he stared out the window at the clouds and dreamed of snow.

CHAPTER 4

MEANWHILE, OUTSIDE THE WINDOW...

A dangerous-looking snow pea named Avalanche crouched in the bushes outside the Asparagus home. He positioned a large microphone right next to the window. Then he ran a thick wire from the microphone out to the street.

Parked on the street was a white van with tinted windows. It read Unmarked Van Rental— When You Need to Not Be Noticed. Dozens of thick wires ran from the neighborhood houses to the van. Avalanche quickly hopped inside with his wire, slamming the door behind him.

Inside the van sat two other snow peas, the aggressive Frostbite and the oversized (but somewhat dim) Snowflake. Avalanche plugged the wire into the side of a large radio console that filled the back of the van. Frostbite put on a pair of headphones.

"It's a little asparagus kid," Frostbite said. "He's telling his dad that he hopes it snows."

"Ooh," said Snowflake. "I like snow."

"He's just like every other kid on the block," Frostbite said. "They all want a snow day, so they won't have to go to school."

"Gee," said Snowflake. "I liked school."

"You did *not*," said Avalanche.

"Sure I did," Snowflake insisted. "Why do you think I spent five years in first grade?"

"Quiet, you two," said Frostbite. "The leader is calling in."

Frostbite hit a button on the console. A menacing voice cackled over the loudspeaker.

"Good work, gentlemen," said the gravelly voice. "I have been monitoring the transmissions from the microphones you set up."

"Thank you, sir," said Frostbite. "All the children want a snow day."

"Of course they do," intoned the voice. "And soon I will use that desire to trick the children into helping us. And when they do, we will turn all of Bumblyburg into a frozen wasteland! Bwaa-haaa-haaa!"

The evil laugh echoed in the van.

"BWAA-HAAA-HAAA!" laughed Frostbite.

"BWAA-HAAA-HAAA!" laughed Avalanche.

"BWAA-HAAA-HAAA?" said Snowflake. "I don't get it."

Snowflake often didn't get it. So he did what he always did when he didn't get it: he pulled out a comic book and waited for the others to stop laughing.

CHAPTER 5

OH, THOSE GOLDEN-RULE DAYS

The auditorium was packed with superheroes, all craning their necks to see the stage. A hush fell over the crowd as Bok Choy, the wise professor, stepped up to the podium.

"Superheroes and superheroes-in-training," Bok Choy began, "you are all gathered here this day to witness an event that has never happened before in our school. We are giving a diploma to a trainee *before* he finishes all of his classes!"

The crowd erupted in cheers. Some of the heroes began to chant, **"LARRYBOY! LARRYBOY!"**

Bok Choy called for quiet.

"That's right," the professor said. "Larryboy is so naturally gifted, so scholastically stupendous, so downright super, he doesn't need to attend classes anymore. There is nothing more for him to learn!"

The crowd once again began their chant. Larryboy, urged on by the crowd, made his way toward the stage. Bok Choy handed him a diploma, which Larryboy graciously accepted.

"Thank you, fellow superheroes. It is a great privilege…"
he began, but someone was interrupting. Larryboy
scanned the crowd for this unwanted intruder.

"Larryboy, wake up!"

"Aw, peanut brittle," he mumbled, as he awoke from his
dream.

THE REAL CHAPTER FIVE...
NOT THE DREAM

Larryboy was sitting at his desk in class. He was taking 'Superhero 101: The Basics of Being Super' at the Bumblyburg Community College. The drowsy cucumber could see Bok Choy lecturing at the front of the room. His classmate, Scarlet Tomato, leaned closer.

"Larryboy," Scarlet whispered, "wake up!"

"I'm awake," Larryboy insisted. "In fact, I wasn't sleeping at all."

"Yes, you were," said the red heroine. "You were snoring."

"Was not," Larryboy replied.

"Were to."

"I wasn't snoring," Larryboy said, trying to think fast. "I was practicing Morse code. With snorts."

"Really?" asked Scarlet Tomato.

"Yep. Pretty good, huh? **SNORT! SNORT! SNORT!**" Larryboy made an obnoxious noise through his nose. "That, my friend, is the letter s."

Scarlet Tomato looked at Larryboy with disbelief.

"Okay, I was sleeping. I'm sorry," Larryboy confessed.

"Well, sleeping or practicing, you've missed the lecture."

That much was true. Bok Choy was just finishing.

"And that," he concluded, "is how I defeated the Snow King! Class dismissed."

The superheroes packed up their books and headed out.

"Except," called Bok Choy, "for Larryboy."

"Oops," said Larryboy.

"Tough break," Lemon Twist called out. The other heroes just giggled. Larryboy walked to the front of the classroom.

"Yes, Professor Choy?" Larryboy asked.

Bok Choy looked meaningfully at the young hero. Larryboy was too embarrassed to look his teacher in the eye.

"Were you sleeping in my class?" asked Bok Choy.

"No, of course not. Don't be silly. Well, maybe a little."

"Son, someday you will realize how important an education is," the teacher said. "When that day comes, you will wish you hadn't slept through so many lectures."

"Yes, sir," said Larryboy.

"You can go."

"Thank you, Professor Choy," said Larryboy. The embarrassed cucumber hurried out of the room.

CHAPTER 6

THE RIDE HOME

VROOOM! Larryboy raced his Larrymobile toward home. Suddenly, his videophone chirped. Archibald, Larryboy's butler, appeared on the video screen.

"Good evening, Master Larry," said Archibald.

"Hello, Archie," muttered the cucumber.

"And how was class this evening?" asked his butler.

"Class?" said Larryboy. "Stimulating. Invigorating. Awe-inspiring."

"Oh?" asked Archibald. "So you fell asleep again?"

"Maybe," Larryboy admitted. "But it wasn't my fault. The lecture was really boring. In fact, school is boring."

"But school can be so much fun," said Archibald. "There are so many good things to learn. I love attending classes."

"I don't," said Larryboy. "I'm an accomplished superhero. I know so much already, I don't need any more schooling. Besides, I have more important things to do with my time."

"Like what?"

"Like playing Tic-Tac-Toe on our Larrycomputer," said Larryboy. "Tonight, I think I can win!"

Archibald sighed as Larryboy clicked off the videophone. "And when it comes to trying to teach you something, Master Larry, it seems I can never win."

CHAPTER 7

THE ICE PLOT THICKENS

"After all, I'm a mature elementary-school kid; I have no more need for schooling." Junior Asparagus stood in the middle of the clubhouse to make his announcement. Laura Carrot, Percy Pea, and Renee Blueberry applauded.

"Me too," said Laura. "I'm sure I've learned all there is to know, at least all that I *need* to know."

"Me too," said Percy. "I've learnt lots."

"That's 'learned,'". corrected Laura.

"I already know how to speak French and English," said Renee, an exchange student from France. She liked to remind others that she was bilingual. "That's more than some teachers."

"And I know both English and Pig Latin," Percy offered.

"Pig Latin isn't a real language," said Renee.

"It-tay is-say ooh-tay," Percy replied.

"We should make a pact," said Junior. "No more school."

"Oui," agreed Renee.

"Yes," said Percy.

"Yeah," Laura chimed in. "Except..."

"Except what?"

Everyone turned to look at Laura.

"Except," she said, "won't we get into trouble?"

"Oh, right," said Junior. "I hadn't thought about that. Does anybody have any other ideas?"

Suddenly there was a knock at the clubhouse door.

"Come in," said Junior.

The door opened. The three snow peas—Avalanche, Frostbite, and Snowflake—stepped into the clubhouse.

"Hello," said one of the snow peas. "My name is Frostbite. These are my brothers, Avalanche and Snowflake."

"Hello," said Junior.

"We aren't supposed to talk with strangers," said Laura.

"Oh, OK," said Snowflake. He turned and walked toward the door, but Avalanche stopped him.

"We'll be going," said Frostbite. "But first, we wanted to tell you kids something."

"What's that?" asked Junior.

"Yeah, what's that?" asked Snowflake.

"We couldn't help overhearing what you were talking about," said Frostbite. "About not wanting to go to school."

"Yeah," said Avalanche. "We heard you wished there was a way to get out of going to school without getting into trouble."

"We tried to be polite and not listen," said Snowflake. "But it was hard not to hear while we were crouching outside your window."

Avalanche gave Snowflake a sharp nudge.

"Ow!" said the snow pea. "What was that for?"

"Anyway," said Frostbite, quickly changing the subject,

"what if we told you that there *is* a way to get out of going to school without getting into trouble? What would you say to that?"

"Wow," said Percy. "For real?"

"No school and no trouble?" asked Laura suspiciously. "I don't believe it."

"Believe it," said Avalanche. "In fact, your parents will be the ones to tell you to stay home."

"No way!" whispered Junior. "But how?"

"You want a snow day, right?" asked Frostbite, mischievously. "Well, we know how you can create your own snow day. And you don't have to wait for winter."

"All you have to do," said Avalanche, "is promise not to tell anyone about it."

The kids looked at each other.

"What do you think, Junior?" asked Renee.

"I don't know," said Junior, looking quite concerned. "It sounds too good to be true."

"But it couldn't hurt to listen to their idea, could it?" asked Percy hopefully.

"Come on, Junior," said Laura, nudging her friend. "A snow day. In September."

"OK," said Junior. "We'll listen. But no promises."

"Of course not," said Frostbite. "Now gather around. And remember, it's a *secret*."

The kids formed a tight circle around Frostbite. They oohed and aahed as they heard the plan—except for Snowflake, who still didn't get it.

CHAPTER 8

BACK AT THE BUMBLE

"Is it dangerous?" Vicki asked. She stood in front of Bob's desk in the editor's office of the *Daily Bumble*.

"It's not dangerous," Bob said. "But it *is* an important assignment, Vicki."

"I was hoping for a dangerous assignment," said Vicki. "All my latest assignments have been a little boring."

"If my information is correct," said the editor, "Bumblyburg won't be boring for long."

Just then there was a knock at the door. Larry, the janitor, stuck his head in.

"Excuse me," said Larry. "I need to clean the ceiling tiles."

"If you have to," said Bob.

Larry entered the room. He attached a squeegee to the end of a long pole and began to wipe the ceiling tiles. Water dripped from his squeegee onto Bob's desk.

"As I was saying," Bob continued, frantically moving his papers this way and that—to avoid the drips. "There is a new supervillain on the loose. His name is Iceberg."

"Iceberg! Really?" asked Larry.

"Really," said Bob, as a drop of water splattered onto his head. "Could you be a little more careful with that squeegee?"

"Sure," said Larry.

"I've heard of him," said Vicki. "His dad was a supervillain back in the days when Bok Choy protected Bumblyburg."

"That's right," said Bob. "Iceberg has been causing trouble with his love of all things cold. He disrupted the big game at the Salad Bowl by creating a hailstorm. And in South Pimento, he froze the mayor's duck pond, turning it into a skating rink!"

"Those poor ducks," sighed Vicki.

"No kidding," said Bob. "Can you imagine how hard it was to find skates that fit webbed feet?"

"So, what's Iceberg up to now?" asked the photographer.

"There is a rumor," said Bob, "that he plans to hit Bumblyburg next!"

"That is a big story," said Vicki. "I'm on it!"

Larry was hanging on to every word. In fact he was listening so carefully that he wasn't watching where he was washing. Before he knew it, the ceiling fan snagged his squeegee, and he was lifted into the air!

"Help!" shouted Larry, as he circled the room.

"Look out!" shouted Vicki, as she ducked in rhythm with the fan blades

"Get down from there!" shouted Bob.

But Larry only spun around faster and faster. He knocked over the books on Bob's bookshelf. He knocked over Bob's lamp. Then he knocked over Bob!

"Ouch," moaned Bob. "Larry!"

"Sorry," said Larry.

CLICK! Larry's spinning slowed to a stop. Vicki had turned off the fan.

"You OK, Boss?" she asked Bob.

"Yeah," Bob said. "Although I can't say the same for our janitor."

Vicki turned toward Larry, who was still clinging to the fan, suspended in midair. The janitor giggled.

"I haven't been this dizzy since I put my overalls in the washer," he said.

"Why would that make you dizzy?" asked Vicki.

"I was still wearing them."

"Are you going to come down from there?" asked Bob.

"I don't know," said Larry. "Are you mad?"

"Yes," said Bob.

"Then I think I'll stay up here awhile."

"Suit yourself," said Bob.

"I'll leave you two alone," said Vicki, quickly leaving the room.

CHAPTER 9

TROUBLE UNDERFOOT WHEN IT RAINS

CLUNK!

Frostbite had just attached a huge metal cylinder to the ceiling of the sewer pipe. He could reach the ceiling because he was standing on top of Avalanche, who was standing on top of Snowflake.

"There. That's the last Mini-Hooha we needed to put into place," Frostbite announced.

"What are Mini-Hoohas anyway?" asked Snowflake.

"These metal gadgets we have been attaching to the ceiling. What do you think?" asked Frostbite. "Now set us down."

Snowflake looked up at the ceiling to study the large cylinder.

"You're leaning back too far!" shouted Frostbite.

"Be careful!" demanded Avalanche.

The two snow peas were leaning perilously to the left. Snowflake shifted his weight. Now his two friends were leaning perilously to the right. Snowflake shifted again.

SPLASH! All three tumbled into the messy

sewer water.

"Yuck!" cried the peas.

"I just spent the whole day putting these gadgets into place," groaned Frostbite, "and now I'm tired and wet. Thanks a lot!"

"Yeah, I was meaning to ask about that," said Snow-flake. "Why did we put all these Mini-Hoohas in the sewer under the streets of Bumblyburg anyway?"

"Listen, freeze brain," said Frostbite, not so nicely. "Each Mini-Hooha is attached to the boss's K.w.a.c.k. machine by these pipes. So when the boss throws the switch, the K.w.a.c.k. will fill up each Mini-Hooha with F.r.i.s.b.e.e.s. Got it?"

"Got it," said Snowflake, but his face revealed that he really didn't.

"Don't worry, Snowflake," said Avalanche. "You'll understand soon enough. That is, if the kids do their part."

"Yeah," said Frostbite. "It's up to the kids now."

...AND RAINS

It was almost midnight. Junior was lying in his bed, staring at the clock. As the second hand approached twelve, he whispered, "Five, four, three, two, one!" Junior jumped out of bed and ran to the door of his bedroom. He carefully pulled the door open and listened. No sounds could be heard from the hallway.

"I sure hope Mom and Dad are asleep," he whispered to himself.

Junior snuck out the door and hopped quietly down the

hall, stopping outside his parents' room to listen.

SNORT.

The loud sound made Junior jump. Were his parents awake?

SHOOOO.

Junior continued to listen.

SNORT. SHOOOO. SNORT. SHOOOO. SNORT. SHOOOO.

It was the sound of snoring! Junior sighed in relief; his parents were definitely asleep. Junior continued down the hall and into the bathroom, quietly closing the door behind him.

"First, the tub," Junior said to himself.

He moved to the tub and put the stopper into the drain. Then he turned on the water. Next, Junior moved to the sink. He put a stopper into the sink drain and turned on the water there too. Quickly hopping back to the door, he opened it and listened.

The only sound was a not-so-soft snoring coming from his parents' room. Junior swiftly moved down the hall and ducked back into his bedroom. He closed his door and hopped into bed.

"Whew!" he sighed. "I wonder how the others are doing?"

...AND RAINS

Down the street from Junior's house, a similar scene was being played out. Laura had just turned on the water at her kitchen sink, when her brother peeked around the corner.

"I got the bathtub going," said Lenny.

"Good job," said Laura.

Then they headed back upstairs.

...AND POURS

Percy Pea lived right around the corner from Laura Carrot. Returning from his bathroom, he hopped back into bed. Then he looked out the window just in time to see the sprinklers on his neighbor's lawn come on. He could see Renee Blueberry as she dashed from the lawn back to her front door. Percy smiled and snuggled down into his bed as he thought about all his other friends turning on the faucets in the neighborhood, too. Everything was going according to plan.

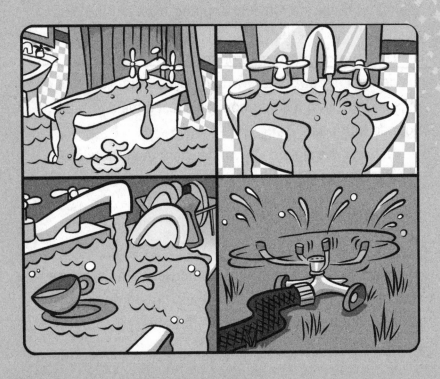

CHAPTER 10

WHERE'S AN ARK WHEN YOU NEED ONE?

Early the next morning, Archibald gently nudged Larry, who was in bed, fast asleep. He was snoring loudly.

"Master Larry," said Archibald. "Please wake up."

"I know the answer," he shouted as he sat up. "I wasn't sleeping!"

"Master Larry, it's me," said Archibald.

"Archie," said Larry. "Why didn't you say so? I thought I was in trouble again."

"You aren't in trouble," assured his butler. "But Bumblyburg *is*. And they need a superhero, right now!"

"They do?" said Larry, getting excited. "I...am... that...hero!"

"Yes, you are," Archibald agreed.

He held out the Larryboy suit, freshly cleaned and ironed, as Larry hopped out of bed and dashed behind the changing screen.

"What seems to be the trouble?" he asked.

"During the night, someone turned on every faucet in Bumblyburg. The whole town is flooded."

"Oh," Larry said, poking

his head around the corner. "Then Bumblyburg doesn't really need a superhero. It sounds like it needs a plumber."

"Perhaps," Archibald admitted. "*If* this was an accident. But Police Chief Croswell suspects foul play."

"Ah, yes," said Larryboy. "This sounds just like the work of 'foul play.'" Larryboy nodded wisely.

Archibald waited, knowing the question would come.

"Who is 'foul play'?" asked Larryboy.

"Perhaps if you would pay more attention in class," said Archibald, "you would know that 'foul play' isn't a person. It means 'an evil plot.'"

"I knew that," said Larry, disappearing behind the screen again.

"Chief Croswell thinks that a supervillain might be attacking Bumblyburg," Archibald went on. "It could be another one of Awful Alvin's schemes or even Plumb Loco."

"Or maybe that ice cube guy that they were talking about at the *Daily Bumble*," suggested Larry.

"Iceberg," corrected Archibald. "Maybe."

"It doesn't matter," said Larry. "None of them is a match for..." Larry jumped out from behind the screen in full uniform. "Larryboy!" he announced.

"Exactly," said Archibald. "And except for the fact that you put your uniform on over your pajamas, you are all set to go."

"Right," said Larryboy, disappearing behind the screen again.

CHAPTER 11

THE ICEBERG COMETH

ZOOM!

Larryboy flew over Bumblyburg
in the Larryplane. The whole town
was indeed flooded, covered knee-deep
in water. Well, knee-deep for average-sized
citizens, like cucumbers and carrots. For shorter
vegetables, like tomatoes and peppers, it was a
whole lot deeper. And for tall Bumblyburgians like
celery, it wasn't as deep. You get the idea.

"Look! There's Officer Olaf," said Larryboy.

Larryboy sent the plane into a dive toward the
street. As the Larryplane neared the ground, the wings
tucked into the sides of the plane and the wheels
popped out. The Larryplane was transformed into the
Larrymobile!

SPLASH! The Larrymobile hit the road, splattering
water everywhere. Our hero splashed up to Officer
Olaf's squad car, sitting in the middle of the road.

"Hey, Olaf!" Larry called.

Officer Olaf rolled down his window.

"Larryboy, am I glad to see you," said the
policeman. "The whole town of Bumblyburg is

flooded. The streets are a mess, and panic is setting in.
People are getting soaked just going out to pick up the
morning paper. And on top of that, the morning papers are
all soggy!"

"I see," said Larryboy.

"And now, even I'm stuck. My engine is flooded!"

"Well," said Larryboy, "you should expect that when
driving in a flood. Kind of silly, don't you think?"

Just then the engine of the Larrymobile sputtered and
died.

"Oops," said our hero. "Sure wish I could get to the Lar-
ryspeedboat!"

"Looks like we are both stuck until the flood subsides,"
said Olaf.

"How long will that be?" asked Larryboy.

"It will take days for the water to drain off."

"It will take longer than that!" A strange voice boomed

across the waters. Larryboy and Olaf looked up and
noticed a van parked directly across the street. The side
door of the van was open. Inside the van was a large,
clear plastic bowl. And sitting in the bowl was...

"Eek! A large head!" screamed Larryboy. "Of lettuce!"

"Looks like the picture of Iceberg on *Bumblyburg's Most
Wanted*," said Olaf.

"That's right," boomed the voice of the lettuce head. "I
am Iceberg, and I'm the new master of the soon-to-be-icy
Bumblyburg!"

"Get him, Larryboy!" shouted Olaf.

"OK!" shouted Larryboy. "Prepare to meet your match,
Iceberg!" Larryboy reached for his door handle.

"It's too late," laughed Iceberg.

And as he laughed, the streets of Bumblyburg began to
shake.

CHAPTER 12

ICE CAPADES

"What's happening?" Officer Olaf had to shout to be heard over the loud rumbling.

"What?" shouted Larryboy. "I can't hear you. You will have to shout to be heard over the loud rumbling."

"I said," shouted Olaf, "what's happening?"

"I am happening," boomed Iceberg. **"BWAA-HAAA-HAAAA!"**

"Hey, I recognize that laugh," said Larryboy. "That is the universal 'evil-menace-to-society' laugh. Only supervillains use that laugh!"

"That's right," Iceberg agreed. "Even now, my machinery is transforming the flood waters of Bumblyburg."

"You're getting rid of the water?" shouted Larryboy. "How thoughtful of you. And I thought you were going to be an evil menace!"

"Not getting rid of," teased Iceberg, "but transforming."

With a loud **CRACK!** the rumbling stopped.

"Glad that's over," said our hero. "Now to see about that head of lettuce."

"Yikes, my door is stuck," said Officer Olaf. "Larryboy, look at the water!"

Larryboy gasped. The water had turned to ice and the Larrymobile was stuck in it. In fact, *all* of Bumblyburg was stuck in ice!

"It worked!" Iceberg crowed. "My plan to turn Bumblyburg into a frozen wasteland has worked!"

"I'll get you for this," Larryboy warned.

"How?" asked the head. "You can't even get out of your car."

"My Larrymobile comes equipped with a special crime-fighting feature made especially for situations like this!"

"What's that?"

"A canopy!" Larryboy quickly popped open the canopy and hopped out onto the ice.

"Not so fast," Iceberg said. He then called out, "Boys!"

ZOOM! ZOOM! ZOOM!

Frostbite, Avalanche, and Snowflake jumped out of the van. Each wore a jet-skate! They zoomed across the ice and encircled Larryboy.

"Only three of you?" taunted Larryboy. "No problem. I can take on all three of you with my arms tied behind my back. If I had arms, that is." The super cucumber hopped toward Frostbite. But he promptly slipped on the ice and fell down.

"Nice try," taunted Frostbite.

"Oh, yeah?" Larryboy responded. He quickly leaped back up to a standing position—and just as quickly slid into a lying-down position.

"This is embarrassing," the cucumber moaned.

"Can't catch us if you can't even stand up," Avalanche teased.

"Oh, yeah?"

POP! Larryboy shot one of his plunger ears straight at Avalanche.

PLOP! It stuck to the snow pea!

"Who's laughing now?" asked our hero.

Avalanche zoomed away from Larryboy. The rope attached to the plunger ear became taut. **SWOOSH!** Just like a water-skier, Larryboy was pulled across the ice!

HMMM, thought Larryboy. **THIS ISN'T EXACTLY WHAT I HAD IN MIND.**

"Hey, fellows," shouted Avalanche. "Let's play whiplash!"

Frostbite and Snowflake glided over to Avalanche, hooked themselves together, and zoomed across the ice, with Larryboy in tow. Then they came to a sudden stop! Larryboy whipped past the trio.

"AAAAHHHH!" screamed Larryboy. Our hero continued sliding until he hit the wall of the Bumblyburg Library. Larryboy slid down the wall in a daze.

"That was fun," said Snowflake.

"Let's do it again!" suggested Avalanche.

"Yippee!" said Frostbite.

The three took off at high speed. Soon, the dazed Larryboy was skiing behind them again.

"Mommy."

"Larryboy!" shouted Officer Olaf. "Release the plunger!"

"What?" shouted Larryboy.

"Release the plunger!"

"Good idea," replied the hero. He turned his head to the side.

POP! The plunger popped off of Avalanche. But too late! The three had already stopped, and Larryboy whipped on past, heading straight for Iceberg's van!

"Look out!" shouted the cucumber.

CRASH! Larryboy flew through the van door and smacked into the wall.

"Hello, Larryboy. I appreciate your dropping by," the villain said. "You don't look so good."

"Eep," said Larryboy.

"And to think I was afraid you would spoil my plans," laughed Iceberg.

"Eep," said Larryboy.

"Well, just to make sure you don't crack this ice capade, you can come and stay with me!" said Iceberg, as he slammed the door shut. Avalanche zoomed to the van and jumped into the driver's side. The engine revved to life, and the van zoomed across the ice.

"Hey, look!" shouted Olaf. "The van was really a rocket-sled in disguise!"

"Nice detective work," Frostbite teased Olaf, skating right up to the police cruiser.

"I hope you have learned something in all of this," the snow pea taunted.

"Learned something? Like what?" asked Officer Olaf.

"That we control Bumblyburg now. Come on, Snowflake!" Frostbite and Snowflake skated off, laughing.

"Hey, that's not funny," shouted Olaf. "Besides, I know Larryboy! He'll find a way to escape and make you all pay!"

The two villains had disappeared.

"At least, I think he will," added Olaf, not really as sure as he sounded.

CHAPTER 13

SNOW DAY

"Bumblyburg overcome by ice!" Junior leaned into the radio as the announcer continued the broadcast.

"Larryboy disappeared while battling Iceberg and his henchmen," the announcer said.

"Police continue their search. In the meantime, all vehicles are advised to stay off the roads. This includes cars, mopeds, motorized pogo sticks, and school buses. So until further notice, school is canceled."

"Wahoo!" Junior flicked off the radio and ran to the front hall. He threw on his coat, hat, and scarf, and raced out the door. His sled was waiting on the porch, where he had left it earlier. He had been pretty confident school would be canceled!

"Just when you thought a day couldn't get any better!" Junior looked up at the falling snow. The weather report had called for rain all morning, but the extreme cold caused by the Bumblyburg ice turned the rain into snow. The entire town was blanketed in white.

The streets were full of kids. Some had

sleds, some ice skates. A snowman was already in progress on the corner. A snowball fight was brewing on the other end of the block.

"Hey, Junior!" Laura Carrot was waving from the street. Percy and Renee stood beside her. Laura pulled a toboggan. Percy and Renee each had snowboards.

"Hey, Laura."

"We're heading to Mortimer's Run. Want to come?" asked Percy.

"You bet," said Junior. The foursome headed up the hill.

"Pretty cool, the ice and all, huh?" asked Percy.

"And no one suspects a thing!" said Renee.

"I wonder," said Junior.

"About what?" asked Laura.

"Well, they say that Larryboy tried to stop Iceberg. Why would Larryboy do that, unless something was wrong?"

"What do you mean?" asked Percy. "We get a snow day, and no one got hurt. What could be wrong?"

"Nothing, I guess," agreed Junior.

"Let's race," said Laura. "Last one to the top of the hill is a rotten tomato!"

"Or a brown banana," chimed Renee.

"Or an apple when it gets those spots that are kind of mushy and…" Percy noticed that the others weren't listening. Instead, they were already speeding away.

"Hey, wait for me!" he cried.

Laughing, the children raced to the top of the hill.

CHAPTER 14

INTO EVERYONE'S LIFE A LITTLE GLOATING MUST FALL

"That was so easy!" Iceberg sat in his bowl in the middle of his hideout. Frostbite, Avalanche, and Snowflake stood around him, listening.

"As slick as ice," said Frostbite.

"As smooth as snow," said Avalanche.

"As orange as my cat," said Snowflake.

The other villians stared at the snow pea in confusion.

"What? My cat is orange," explained Snowflake.

"Anyway," said Iceberg, with a scowl, "my plan took place without a hitch. The kids played their parts perfectly."

"What irony," said Frostbite. "Bumblyburg's own kids helped us out."

"And we skated circles around the local law enforcement," said Avalanche.

"Actually, I did more of a figure eight," said Snowflake.

"And Bumblyburg's superhero is just a superjoke," said Iceberg.

"I heard that!" said Larryboy. The cucumber sat forlorn in his ice cage.

"I wanted you to hear that," jeered the master villain.

"Well, you won't get away with this," said Larryboy.

"I already did," laughed Iceberg. "In fact, I accomplished what my father, the Snow King, could never do. I conquered Bumblyburg!"

"Yeah, well, you won't get away with this for much longer," said Larryboy. "I'm a trained superhero. We are taught to take care of villains like you."

"Oh, yeah?" replied Iceberg. "And just what did they teach you?"

"Stuff," said Larryboy. "I just don't remember it right now."

"Hah!" Iceberg gloated. "A superhero that doesn't pay attention in class."

"I don't need to pay attention in class," Larryboy retorted. "I don't need classes to defeat you."

"I wish you would be quiet," said Iceberg. "You're ruining my celebration party."

"I'll take care of him," said Frostbite. "Hey, pickle-boy."

"I'm not a pickle-boy," said Larryboy. "I'm a cucumber-boy."

"Whatever. I dare you to stick your tongue to the ice bar of your cage."

"That's silly," said Larryboy. "Why would I do that?"

"Are you chicken?" taunted Frostbite.

"No, I'm a cucumber," said Larryboy.

"Prove it," said Frostbite.

"OK," said Larryboy, sticking his tongue against the bar.

"Thee? No pwobwem."

But when Larryboy tried to pull his tongue back into his mouth, it was stuck!

"Hey," he said, "my thongue ith thtuck!"

Iceberg and the snow peas laughed.

"Dowen waff," lisped Larryboy. "Ith na thunny!"

But the villains laughed even louder because, to be honest, it was funny.

CHAPTER 15

MUCH LATER

"Wow, a whole week without school. This is great!" Junior said. He and his friends were on their way to the clubhouse.

"Yeah, a whole week of sledding," said Percy.

"It sure is fun," agreed Renee. "Isn't it?

"Of course it is," said Percy.

When they entered the clubhouse, Laura was already there, reading. But as her friends entered, Laura hid her book.

"What are you doing, Laura?" asked Junior.

"Nothing," she said.

"It looked like you were reading," said Renee.

"How was sledding?" asked Laura.

"Got it!" Percy shouted. He had sneaked behind Laura and was holding up her book. "A math book!"

"So I was reading a math book," said Laura. "So what?"

"So we aren't going to school all week," said Junior. "You don't have to look at math."

"What if I wanted to?"

"Why would you want to do *that*?" asked Renee.

"To me, math problems are like puzzles," said Laura. "And without school, well, I miss doing them. I guess I like math."

"I can't believe it," said Percy. "She misses math!"

"What's wrong with that?" demanded Laura.

"If you are going to miss anything," Percy teased, "it should be reading."

"You miss reading?" asked Junior.

"Don't you?" Percy responded. "I'm a pretty good reader. And there are lots of cool stories out there. I was kinda looking forward to reading another one."

"Someday, you will be reading *my* books," said Renee. "When I grow up, I'm going to be a famous author."

"For real?" asked Percy.

"For real," said Renee. "Of course, I still have to learn how to become a good writer."

"When I grow up, I'm going to be an engineer," said Junior.

"You'll need to know a lot of math to be an engineer," said Laura.

"I will?"

"Of course."

"Gee, what if Bumblyburg *stays* frozen and we don't ever get to go back to school? Then I'll never get to be an engineer," said Junior.

"And I'll never become a writer," said Renee.

"Maybe school wasn't so bad after all," suggested Junior.

"I miss art class too," said Laura. "Especially painting."

"I really liked gym class," said Percy.

There was a long pause. "I think we may have made a mistake," said Junior.

"Do you think so?" asked Percy.

"I do," said Junior. "My dad told me that when you stop learning, you stop growing. He said that God wants us to keep learning, even after we grow up. I think we have disappointed him. And maybe a whole lot of other people too."

"I think you're right, Junior," said Laura. "We never should have helped those snow peas."

"Now we'll never be able to go back to school!" cried Percy.

"What can we do?" asked Renee.

"There's only one thing we *can* do," said Junior. "We have to find Larryboy. Then he can help us make things right again."

CHAPTER 16

FOLLOW THAT VILLAIN!

"Can't catch me! Can't catch me!" Frostbite taunted Officer Olaf and Chief Croswell.

The two police officers tried to grab the villain as he skated around them on his jet-skate. But both officers had trouble keeping their balance on the ice. Frostbite came to a stop close to Olaf.

"Catch me high!" the snow pea taunted.

Officer Olaf grabbed for Frostbite, but the villain zoomed away too quickly. He skated near Croswell.

"Catch me low!" he yelled at the policeman.

Croswell reached out, but again Frostbite zoomed off before he could be nabbed. The snow pea came to a halt directly in between Olaf and Croswell.

"Catch me in the middle!" he shouted.

"I've got him!" yelled Olaf as he dove for Frostbite.

"No, I've got him!" yelled Croswell, jumping for Frostbite from the opposite direction. Croswell and Olaf almost reached Frostbite at the same time, but the snow pea zoomed away at the last second.

BAM!

Olaf and Croswell smashed into each other. They spun around on the ice, landing in a pile.

"Much too slow!" yelled Frostbite. Laughing, he zoomed away.

"Look, there goes Frostbite," whispered Junior to Laura, Percy, and Renee. The four of them were at the top of a hill, looking down on the streets.

"Larryboy was last seen with Iceberg and the snow peas," he continued. "If we follow him, we might find Larryboy."

"Wouldn't that be dangerous?" asked Renee.

"I'm not sure about this," said Percy, nervously.

"I'm with you, Junior," said Laura, with a determined look.

"If we don't want to lose him, we have to go now," Junior said. Junior jumped onto his sled. **SWOOSH!** He sailed down the hill, in pursuit of Frostbite.

"Let's go!" Laura yelled as she jumped onto her toboggan. Percy and Renee followed on their snowboards.

"Wheee!" shouted Renee.

"Shush!" shushed Laura.

"Sorry," whispered Renee, before letting out one last little "Whee!"

CHAPTER 17

STICKY SITUATION

"Larryboy? Can you hear me?" Archibald was speaking through the radio in Larryboy's suit.

"Larryboy, can you hear me?"

"Althred, ith thad you?"

"Larryboy, I'm having trouble understanding you. Did you stick your tongue to the ice bars again?"

"He double dared me," Larryboy said.

"Haven't you learned your lesson about that? You have to stop taking their dares," Archibald told him. "Listen, I am working on a plan to defeat Iceberg. I need you to be patient."

"I'll be bathiend," Larryboy mumbled.

"Who are you talking to?" Snowflake asked as he came over to the cage.

"No one," said Larryboy.

"No one what?" asked Archibald.

"I'b na dalging do anyone," said Larryboy.

"Good, 'cause I don't want any trouble from you," said Snowflake. "Iceberg left me in charge when he and the boys went to town."

"Day wend do down?" asked Larryboy.

"Who went to town?" asked Archibald.

"Arthy, I'm buthy," slurred Larryboy.

"Oh, sorry," said the butler. "I'll call back later."

"What did you say?" said Snowflake.

"Day wend do down?" repeated Larryboy.

"Yes," said Snowflake, "to send off a letter to Iceberg's father. He is the Snow King, you know—a very powerful supervillain."

"Da No King?"

"That's right."

DING-DONG. They were interrupted as the doorbell to the secret hideout rang.

"That's funny," said Snowflake. "My pizza shouldn't be here for another half an hour." Snowflake left the room to answer the door.

"Psst, Larryboy!" Junior and Laura snuck out from behind the door.

"Hetho, Thunior an Wauwa," said Larryboy. "How'd do ged here?"

"We snuck in the back. Renee and Percy are distracting Snowflake at the front door," said Laura. "We don't have much time. We have to get you out of here."

"Bud I'm thuck," said Larryboy.

"I've got just the thing," said Junior. "We can use the hot chocolate I brought for a snack."

The small asparagus opened a thermos and poured some of the hot chocolate onto Larryboy's tongue.

The superhero pulled himself free. "Thanks," he said. "Freedom tastes good!"

"And now the lock," said Junior. He poured the remaining cocoa on the lock of the ice cage. The lock melted, and Larryboy hopped out of the cage.

"What are you kids doing here?" asked the superhero.

"We had to help," said Laura. "This is all our fault. We kids helped Iceberg turn Bumblyburg into an ice world."

"Why would you do that?" Larryboy asked.

"We wanted a snow day, so we wouldn't have to go to school," said Junior. "But we've learned our lesson."

"Yeah, we actually *miss* school," admitted Laura. "Some of it, anyway."

"Really?" asked Larryboy.

"Yeah," said Junior. "My dad was right: when you stop learning, you stop growing."

"Hey!" said Larryboy. "That reminds me of something. My teacher at school talked about the Snow King."

"Who's the Snow King?" the kids asked in unison.

"He was a supervillain that Bok Choy defeated. And he's Iceberg's dad!"

"Really?" asked Junior.

"Bok Choy told us how he defeated the Snow King. Maybe we can defeat Iceberg in the same way."

"What did your teacher say?" asked Laura.

"He said...he said..." stammered Larryboy. "I don't know what he said. I wasn't paying attention."

"Let's find Bok Choy and ask him," said Junior.

"Good idea," said Larryboy.

"Quick," said Laura. "Let's go out the back way before Snowflake returns."

The trio quickly raced out the back. And not a moment too soon! Snowflake walked into the room, carrying a small box.

"Guess what," he said. "That wasn't my pizza at all. But I did manage to buy a box of Veggie Scout cookies. Do you like thick mints?"

Snowflake looked at the empty cage. "Oh, no! Larryboy is gone!" Snowflake looked around the room.

"That can mean only one thing," he said. "More cookies for me!"

CHAPTER 18

BACK TO SCHOOL

"And that is why, class, we need to be humble heroes," Bok Choy lectured a young group of superheroes. Unlike the Bumblyburg Elementary School, the superhero college was still in session.

Suddenly the door burst open, and Larryboy hopped in. "Emergency, Professor Choy!" yelled Larryboy.

"Speaking of humble heroes," Bok Choy said calmly. "Class, let me introduce you to Larryboy."

"Hello, Mr. Larryboy!" recited the class in unison.

"Now then," said Bok Choy. "What is your emergency?"

"Iceberg has turned all of Bumblyburg into ice," said Larryboy. "We must stop him!"

"And why are you telling me?" asked the teacher.

"Well," said Larryboy, "the Snow King is Iceberg's father. And since you defeated the Snow King, I thought you might be able to tell me how I could defeat Iceberg."

"I see," said Bok Choy. "You want me to teach you about the Snow King?"

"Sure," said the superhero.

"Wasn't my last lecture all about the Snow King?"

"Uhm," stuttered the cucumber. "Yeah, but…"

"But you weren't paying attention," frowned Bok Choy. "Maybe this time you will."

Bok Choy went to the front of the room. He drew on the chalkboard for a moment. When he stepped back, he showed the class a complex diagram.

"Now then," he said. "When the Snow King tried to turn Bumblyburg into a frozen wasteland, he used a K.w.a.c.k." Bok Choy pointed to a box on the board.

"A kwack?" asked Larryboy. "Quick, what's a kwack?"

"A King-sized Winterizing Auto-Compression Kalvinator. It's a large freezing machine."

"Got it," said Larryboy. "Are we done?"

"Not hardly," said his teacher. "The K.w.a.c.k. was connected to a hundred different Mini-Hoohas, which he had installed in the sewer system."

"Minihaha?"

"Mini-Hooha," Bok Choy responded. "Miniature Heat Oscillation Obfuscating Hydro-freon Accelerator."

"Oh," said Larryboy. "One of those. I'm running out of time. Can you just tell me how to stop Iceberg?"

"I am teaching you about Iceberg's methods," said the wise professor. "It is through learning that you will find the solution."

"But it's not time for *my* class," said Larryboy. "Can't we just jump to the answer?"

"Learning requires much more than simply obtaining answers," said Bok Choy. "It is also about wisdom. Whether you are in the classroom or in life, whether you are young or old, when you stop learning—you stop growing. Larryboy, can you tell me what the superhero handbook says in section 20, paragraph 9, subsection 9?"

Larryboy shrugged his shoulders. Bok Choy turned to the students in the classroom.

"Class?" he asked.

The students all spoke in unison. "Instruct a wise man and he will be wiser still; teach a righteous man and he will add to his learning," they chanted.

"That's right," said the teacher. "Larryboy, listen, learn, and grow. It's all part of becoming wiser."

Bok Choy turned back to the diagram on the chalkboard.

"Now then, where was I?" he asked. "Ah, yes. Snow King had each of these Mini-Hoohas wired to the K.w.a.c.k. machine. And when the K.w.a.c.k. was turned on, it pumped out compressed F.r.i.s.b.e.e.s. to each Mini-Hooha. F.r.i.s.b.e.e.s. was Snow King's special creation, a super freezing liquid called Freon Reactivated Ionizing Sodium Bicarbonate Energy Evaporation Solution. Understand?"

"Understand what?" asked Larryboy, looking up in surprise. "Yes. Hoohas. Frisbees. Cold."

"Right."

"So how did you stop the Snow King?" the cucumber asked.

"Simple," said Bok Choy. "I turned off the K.w.a.c.k."

"Simple!" said Larryboy. After a pause, Larryboy asked sheepishly, "Where do I find the k.w.a.c.k. again?"

Bok Choy sighed. "It takes tremendous power to make all the machines work," said Bok Choy. "Such power will give off readings on the Energy Spectrograph. Simply find a large energy drain. That should lead you to the K.w.a.c.k. machine."

"Got it!" Larryboy hopped out of the room. Seconds later, he popped his head back in.

"And thanks! This whole learning thing seems like a pretty good idea," he admitted. Then he was gone.

CHAPTER 19

A NEW LARRYTOY

Larryboy hurried out into the school parking lot. Junior, Laura, Percy, and Renee were waiting for him.

"Hey, kids," Larryboy yelled, "I figured out what we need to do."

"Larryboy, look at this!" Junior shouted.

Larryboy looked out into the parking lot where Archibald, his butler, stood among the kids.

"Hey, Archie, what are you doing here?"

In answer, Archie simply pointed. There sat the Larrymobile. But not the usual Larrymobile. Instead, it was the Larry*snow*mobile! The car had been converted to a snowmobile, with treads in the place of the back wheels and skis up front.

"Cool!" said Larryboy, his eyes sparkling.

"I thought this might help," said Archie. "I also have a new uniform for you." Archibald brandished a snowsuit version of the Larryboy costume. "It's insulated to keep you warm. And it has traction grips to keep you from falling on the ice."

"Nifty! Thanks," Larryboy said. He grabbed the new suit and jumped inside it.

"Wait," said Archibald. "There are a few more features…"

"I don't have time to learn about new features," said Larryboy, his face set in determination.

"You don't have *time* to learn?" Archibald cocked his eyebrow. "Where have I heard that before?"

"I have to quickly find Iceberg's kwack doodad and the Frisbee juice, so I can turn it off," explained the cucumber.

"Kwack doodad?" asked Junior.

"Frisbee juice?" questioned Laura.

The kids leaned forward in excitement.

"Yep," said the superhero. "Bok Choy said that the kwack thingy uses a lot of energy. And that energy drain should show up on an Energy Spectacle-something."

"Do you mean an Energy Spectrograph?" asked Archibald.

"That's exactly right," said Larryboy with surprise.

"I have one of those in the Larrycave," said the butler.

"Great, then off we go to the Larrycave! I'm outta here!" Larryboy revved up the Larrysnowmobile and zoomed off.

"Larryboy, wait!" called Archibald. But it was too late. Larryboy was gone. "Oh, my."

"Let's follow him," said Junior. "He still might need our help."

The other kids agreed.

"Say, Master Junior?" asked Archibald.

"Yes, sir?"

"I don't suppose you could give me a lift?"

"Sure, hop on," the youngster said.

Archibald slipped onto the back of Junior's sled, and

they slid off down the hill.

CHAPTER 20

OF SNOWBALLS AND SNOW PEAS

"There it is!" said Larryboy.

Larryboy and the kids crouched on a hill, looking down at an igloo. Frostbite, Avalanche, and Snowflake stood outside.

"Archie says the Spector-thingymabob indicated this is the spot," said Larryboy.

"I bet the snow peas are guarding the K.w.a.c.k. machine," said Junior.

"Hmmm." Larryboy thought for a moment. "I'll need a distraction to get inside."

"We've got just the thing," said Laura. "Ready, kids?"

"Ready!"

The foursome jumped on their sled, toboggan, and snowboards and zoomed down the hill. Each had a pile of snowballs.

"Hey, pea pods!" Junior yelled. "Snowball fight!"

The kids pelted the villains with snowballs as they zoomed past and continued down the hill past the igloo.

"What do those kids think they are doing?" snarled Frostbite.

"I'll teach them," growled Avalanche.

"Snowball fight? Cool!" said Snowflake.

The three snow peas fired up their jet-skates and took off after the kids. As soon as they were gone, Larryboy zoomed up in his Larrysnowmobile, hopped out and quickly entered the igloo.

CHAPTER 21

OFF KILTER

It wasn't too hard to
locate the King-sized Winterizing
Auto-Compression Kalvinator. A large
machine stood in the middle of the room.
Red, yellow, and blue lights blinked all over
the machine like a Christmas tree gone mad. On
top of the contraption, sparks jumped between two
antennae, making a loud **ZAP** with each spark. The
contraption roared and groaned and clunked, making
an incredible racket.

"Hmmm," said Larryboy. "I wonder how you turn
this thing off."

Then he noticed a big switch on the side of the
machine. The switch was labeled On and Off. It was
currently in the On position.

"No, too easy," said Larryboy. "But it can't hurt to try."
Larryboy pulled the switch to Off. Slowly, the
roars, groans, and clunks ground to a halt. The yellow lights stopped blinking, then the red, and then
the blue. The antennae at the top of the machine
threw a final spark, and the last **ZAP** echoed in
the room. The machine was off!

"I did it," he said. "I did it! I did it!"

Larryboy ran out of the igloo.

"I did it! We've won! We've..." That's when Larryboy noticed that the ice was still there.

"Hey, if I turned off the doodad, why isn't the ice melting?"

"I'm glad you asked," smiled Iceberg.

Larryboy spun around. Iceberg sat in his plastic bowl just behind the hero.

"Hey, I learned how to defeat you!" shouted Larryboy.

"You learned how to defeat my father," Iceberg corrected.

"It will work on you too," said Larryboy. "Won't it?"

"Not if I have learned more about my father's failure than you have," said the head of lettuce. "He was defeated when his K.w.a.c.k. was turned off. So I made a few changes. Once the K.w.a.c.k. feeds F.r.i.s.b.e.e.s. to my Mini-Hoohas, they are able to keep freezing for a long time. Time enough for me to turn the K.w.a.c.k. on again."

"Not if I put you in jail first!" Larryboy warned, turning his head to the side.

POP! Larryboy hurled one of his plunger ears toward Iceberg. But before it could hit, Frostbite moved in front of him! **PLOP!** The plunger stuck to Frostbite.

"Fool," said Iceberg. "You didn't think those children could distract my team for long, did you?"

Larryboy followed Iceberg's gaze. Avalanche and Snowflake stood beside Junior, Laura, Renee, and Percy. The kids were tied up!

"Take care of him, gentlemen," Iceberg commanded. "And then take care of those annoying children!"

Frostbite, Avalanche, and Snowflake looked menacingly at Larryboy.

"Uh-oh," said Larryboy.

CHAPTER 22

WHIPLASH!

"Want to go for a ride?" Frostbite asked. "Come on, boys!"

The three snow peas hooked up and zoomed off together. They pulled Larryboy behind them; faster and faster they went. Then **WHOOSH!** The trio came to a sudden stop. Larryboy was whipped past them and hurtled toward a snow bank!

Hmmm, thought our hero. *This is like déjà vu all over again.*

"Larryboy, come in Larryboy," Archibald was calling on Larryboy's helmet radio.

"I'm a little busy, Archie," said Larryboy. "I'm being whiplashed."

"Then use your snow-brake!"

"What snow-brake?"

"The one I installed in your new costume. Turn your head to the right twice."

Larryboy tried turning his head, but he was so dizzy from being whiplashed that he didn't know his right from his left! Suddenly, he heard music and singing.

"*He's bigger than Godzilla or the monsters on TV. Oh...*"

"Alfred!" screeched Larryboy.

"The right, Master Larry, the *right!*" Alfred shouted. "Turning your head to the left turns on the radio."

Larryboy turned his head the other direction twice. A metal claw popped out of the back of his costume and dug into the ice. Larryboy came to an immediate stop.

"Cool," said the hero. "And now it's the snow peas' turn!" Larryboy twisted his body around. The rope on the plunger ear became taut.

"Uh-oh," said Frostbite, as he was pulled backward. Avalanche and Snowflake, still attached to Frostbite, were also being pulled backward.

"How about doing circles, boys!" Larryboy taunted. Using his brake as traction, the hero spun in a circle. At the other end of the rope, the three snow peas slid round and round as Larryboy made them go faster and faster.

"Now it's time for a ride!" **POP!** Larryboy released the plunger ear. The three snow peas flew off, skating out of control.

BAM! Frostbite smashed into a snowdrift.

BAM! Avalanche smashed into Frostbite.

"Look out, I'm going to... Oh never mind!" shouted Snowflake as—**BAM!**—he smashed into the other two. The three lay in a heap on the snowdrift.

"Now it's your turn, Iceberg," Larryboy said, turning to Iceberg. **POP!** Larryboy sent his ear toward the villain.

PLOP! It stuck right to Iceberg's container!

"Try getting out of this one," said Larryboy.

"OK," said Iceberg, as his container began to hum.

"What's that?" asked Larryboy.

"Oh, I have a few tricks of my own," boasted the head of lettuce. "My bowl comes with its own Mini-Hooha. Right now I am supercooling the air around me!"

Larryboy noticed that his plunger ear had frosted over. **CRACK!** The plunger shattered into pieces.

"You see," said the villain, "anything that I get close to will freeze and shatter. Watch as I get closer to you."

A series of jet rockets attached to the villain's bowl roared to life. The bowl rose into the air as cold air swirled about him. Using the jets, Iceberg zoomed toward Larryboy. As he came closer, the rope that ran to the plunger frosted over and splintered into pieces.

"Peanut brittle!" said Larryboy.

"No...ice brittle..." said the villain, as Iceberg hovered closer and closer.

CHAPTER 23

ICEBERG OFF THE STARBOARD BOW

Larryboy could feel the air getting colder as Iceberg approached.

"Look!" he shouted. "A salad shooter!"

"Where?" Iceberg shrieked as he turned to look.

"Made you look," mocked Larryboy. He raced around Iceberg and dove for the Larrysnowmobile.

"Oh, no you don't," threatened Iceberg.

He raced after Larryboy. But before he could catch up, our hero jumped into his vehicle, fired up the engine, and drove off in his Larrysnowmobile.

"Whew," he said. "That was close!" But glancing into his rearview mirror, Larryboy could see that Iceberg was right behind him! Larryboy sped up, but Iceberg's rockets were powerful. The head of lettuce was right on his tail! Our hero banked left and headed across a field.

"Archie! Archie, are you there?"

The videophone came to life. Archibald looked out at our hero. "Did the snow-brake work?" he asked.

"Yeah, but nothing else has," said Larryboy.

"I turned off the k.w.a.c.k. doodad, but the ice didn't melt. And now Iceberg is on my tail. He's going to freeze me!"

"Well, that *is* a quandary," said Archibald. "Did Bok Choy teach you anything else about Snow King and Iceberg?"

"Well, he was showing me all sorts of stuff," said Larryboy. "But I wasn't paying attention. I only wanted a quick answer."

"Oh, my," said Archibald.

"Why didn't I pay attention? Professor Choy told me that learning was about much more than answers. He told me that if I stopped learning, I'd stop growing. And now I won't ever grow in wisdom again! What kind of superhero have I become?"

"Maybe it isn't all hopeless," said Archibald. "Can you remember *anything* he said at all?"

"Well," said the cucumber. "He had a diagram on the board. It had the K.w.a.c.k. on it."

"What else was on the diagram?"

"Oh, lots of stuff," replied Larryboy. "It was very pretty."

Archibald tried to keep his voice from showing his rising distress. "Can you remember anything *specific* about the diagram?" he asked.

"Yes!" said the hero triumphantly. "Some of it was blue!"

"I mean, anything specific about what he drew!"

"Oh, that," said Larryboy. "Let me think. Oh, yeah. He said the Snow King planted minithingies in the sewer. That's how everything got so cold. **YIKES!**"

Larryboy was heading straight for a tree! He banked

sharply to the right, nearly causing the snowmobile to top-
ple over. Larryboy leaned hard to the left, and the snowmobile plopped back upright.

Larryboy checked his mirror. As Iceberg passed the
tree, it froze over and shattered.

"Iceberg is still right behind me," he reported. "If he
gets too close to me, I'm an instant veggiesicle."

"Oh, dear," said Archibald. "I'm out of ideas."

"Wait!" said Larryboy. "I'm not. Quick, Archie, check
your map of Bumblyburg. I need to find a way into the
city's sewer."

Larryboy checked his rearview mirror again. Iceberg
was gaining on him! Icicles popped in the air around him.
Larryboy tried to think warm thoughts, but he could feel
the air around him growing colder. His plan had to work!

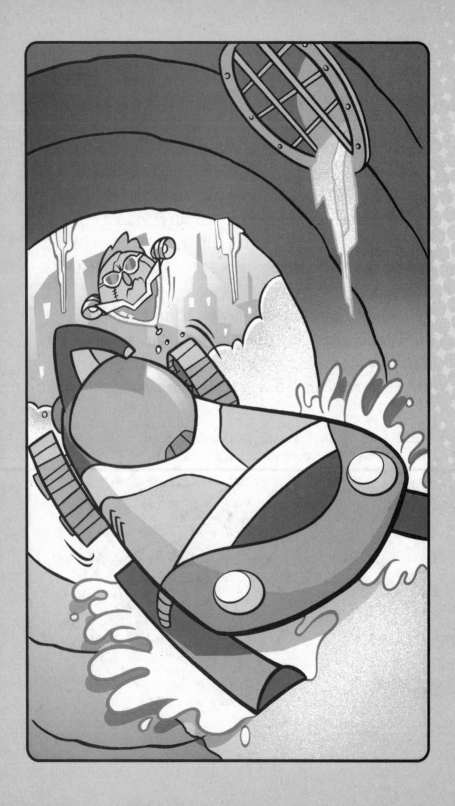

CHAPTER 24

FIFTEEN DEGREES BELOW STREET LEVEL

"Take a left at that tree, Larryboy."

The superhero banked left and zoomed across the field.

"Straight ahead," continued Archibald. "You should see a large pipe. That will get you into the sewer."

"Good job, Archie!" said Larryboy. "Now, keep an eye on the map. You have to make sure I go into every tunnel."

Larryboy zoomed toward the large pipe, but Iceberg was right behind him as the Larrysnowmobile entered the sewer.

"Aagh! I've gone blind," screamed the hero.

"No, you haven't," Archibald reassured him. "It's dark in the tunnels. Turn on your headlights."

Larryboy pushed the white button, and his windshield wipers came to life.

"The green button, Larryboy," said Archibald. "Remember, lime for lights. White for wipers!"

"Right," said Larryboy, as he hit the green button and his headlights came on. **"AAAAHHH!"** he shrieked. He was heading straight for a wall!

"Right! Turn right!" Archibald yelled.

Larryboy swerved right and checked his mirror. He could barely see Iceberg rocketing along, the walls freezing as he passed.

"Take the next left," Archibald said as Larryboy swerved. "Now right and then left again."

Larryboy swerved through the tunnels. Each time he turned, Iceberg turned with him, turn after turn after turn.

"That's it," said Archibald. "Now you just have to… Look out!"

"I have to what?" asked Larryboy. He peered out his front windshield and saw that he was headed straight for another wall! Larryboy slammed on his brakes, and Iceberg skidded to a halt behind him.

"Archie, it's a dead end," Larryboy whispered urgently. "I'm trapped."

"There's a manhole cover above you, leading up to the street," said Archibald.

Larryboy hopped out and stood on top of the Larrysnowmobile. He looked up and saw the manhole cover. But Iceberg was standing right under it!

"There's no escaping now," said Iceberg. "It's time for cucumber ice cream!"

"Not so fast," Larryboy said with a smile. "Hear anything?"

DRIP. DRIP. DRIP. The sound echoed throughout the sewer.

"What's that?" Iceberg asked.

"That is the ice above us melting," said our hero. "Your minithingamabobs have been destroyed."

"My Mini-Hoohas?" Iceberg looked behind him. He could see pieces of the shattered machines lining the floor.

"But...how?" was all he could manage to sputter.

"*You* did it," said Larryboy. "You supercooled everything you came near. While you chased me, I lead you past every minidoohickey you put in the sewer. As you passed them, they shattered to pieces."

"You may have destroyed my Mini-Hoohas," said Iceberg, "but I can still destroy *you*!"

"Maybe," said Larryboy. "But right now there is a ton of water directly above you. And only that metal cover stands between you and the water."

Iceberg looked up at the manhole cover. It was frosted over.

"Looks brittle, doesn't it?" asked Larryboy.

"ARRGH!" yelled Iceberg as he lurched toward the cucumber.

POP! Larryboy shot his remaining plunger ear. It smashed into the manhole cover, and the cover shattered! A flood of water poured down on Iceberg, instantly freezing, which trapped Iceberg in a giant icicle!

"WHEW," said Larryboy. "That was close. Now to get the police to help me defrost this Iceberg!"

CHAPTER 25

THE ICEBERG GOETH

Slam!

Officer Olaf closed
the door on the paddy wagon.
Inside was a soggy Iceberg, looking
rather wilted inside his bowl. At his side
sat Frostbite, Avalanche, and Snowflake. Only
Snowflake looked excited to be there.

"Play the siren, play the siren!" the large snow
pea chanted, as the paddy wagon rode off toward
the Bumblyburg jail.

"Thanks, Larryboy," Officer Olaf said. "Bumblyburg
would still be Bumbly-*Ice*-burg if it hadn't been for
you."

"Well, if I hadn't learned my lesson that learning is a good idea, I'd be a frozen veggie pop. Then
my tongue would stick to my lips all the time. But Bok
Choy was right; you're never too old to keep learning.
When you stop learning, you stop growing."

"Sounds like a wise teacher," said Croswell.

"The kids helped, too," said Larryboy. "I hope
their parents go easy on them." Junior, Laura,
Percy, and Renee stood a few feet away with
their parents, making explanations. They were

shaking in their boots—and this time not from the cold.

"And that's the whole story," said Junior. "We're really sorry."

"Yeah," said Laura. "We sure learned our lesson."

"And what did you learn about playing with the sink?" asked Percy's dad.

"Never, ever plug the drain and leave the water running," Percy repeated.

"Not only did it cause a lot of damage to the house," said Junior, "it's also very dangerous."

"We'll never do it again," said Renee.

"So that's that, right?" asked Percy.

"Not quite," said Percy's mom.

"You still need to be punished for flooding Bumblyburg," said Mr. Asparagus. "We parents have agreed that you are to be suspended for one week."

"For one week," explained Laura's mom, "you can't go to school."

"Can't go to school!" yelled Junior. "That's not fair! We've already lost a week of school."

"Yeah," said Renee. "We miss art and writing."

"And gym and reading," complained Percy.

"And math," added Laura.

"So, you *like* school?" asked Mr. Asparagus.

"Well, sort of," said Junior, embarrassed to admit it.

"A little," said Laura, looking down at her shoes.

"In a way," said Percy. "Sometimes."

"Oui," whispered Renee.

"I see," said Mr. Asparagus, looking at the other parents. They all were smiling. "The punishment is a week of no school. And since you've already missed school, then you've already been punished."

"Really?" asked Junior. "Thanks, Dad."

"Yeah, thanks," said Laura.

"Oui," whispered Renee.

"Looks like my work here is done," said Larryboy. He hopped to the manhole opening and looked down. "Hey, the sewer is flooded!"

"Of course," Chief Croswell said. "Where did you think all the water would go?"

"Well," Larryboy said, "I didn't think that far ahead. I sort of left my Larrysnowmobile parked down there."

"Oh, don't worry. The water will clear out before long."

"How long?"

"About a week."

"A week?" said Larryboy. "I wonder how I'll explain this to Archie."

Larryboy hopped down the street, talking to himself. "Hey, Archie, guess what? You know how you always tell me to take the Larrymobile to the carwash? No, that won't work. Hey, Archie, you know how you keep telling me that walking is good exercise? No, he won't go for that either. Hey, Archie, you know how hard it is to find a parking space downtown? Well, not anymore. No, that's not going to do it. Hey, Archie, you know how I always wanted a Larrysubmarine? Yeah! That one's perfect."

Larryboy's voice trailed off as he disappeared into the distance.

THE END

We want to hear from you. Please send your comments about this book to us in care of zreview@zondervan.com. Thank you.

ZONDERVAN.com/
AUTHORTRACKER
follow your favorite authors